THE Santa Shop
A NOVEL OF HOPE

THE
Santa Shop
A NOVEL OF HOPE

...in our troubled times

TIM GREATON

Published by RKD Press
ISBN 1-58961-036-9

Occasionally, just occasionally, something wonderful happens to someone who doesn't deserve it. In my case, there were four somethings: All my love and thanks to Joan, my wife, and to my three children, Kayla, Brandon and Zachary, whom I have had the pleasure to watch become the amazing young people that they are. A prouder and more thankful husband and dad does not likely exist.

Chapter One

A Holiday of Peace

"Why are you dressed like that?" Karen asked. "It's Christmas not Halloween, you know."

I smiled at her petite reflection barely a step behind my own in the large oval dressing mirror. I finished buttoning the black robe that I had pulled over my normal jeans and flannel shirt. "Saint Nick's in the heart, not the clothes." I turned and drew her to me. "Do you know how much I love you?"

"Yes, but tell me again."

"A whole lot," I said as I gently brushed a lock of brown hair from her forehead and kissed her lips—lips just as sweet and soft as they had been that first time. It was hard to believe that a year and a half had already passed.

When we finally parted, I surveyed the bedroom. The deed to the house and the toyshop were both lying neatly on top of the dresser. Both Karen and I had properly signed and laid them out for David to find when he began moving in the next day. He'd be surprised at the Christmas gift. Though he was expecting to move in, he didn't know we were giving him both the house and the shop.

Five suitcases were lined neatly alongside the recently-made bed. Other than the two, medium-sized boxes in the living room, four of those suitcases represented everything we were taking with us. Karen had already removed our pictures from the wall. I knew she would have taken special care to pack the photos of Tabitha and Derek safely. Both she and I had been vacuuming and cleaning all day and the place looked easily as good as the day we had taken it over.

I glanced outside. The sky was dark and the street lights of the little Vermont town were shining through our windows. This Christmas

Eve other families were likely huddled around their holiday meals, while we, however, were on our way to begin a new life. We were going to miss this wonderful place.

The melody of *Jingle Bells* drifted in from the living room. For weeks now, Karen had been playing Christmas music and even in these, our last few hours in this house, she was appreciating the magic of the season.

"I should be going," I told her.

"I know," she said. "I'll finish things up around here."

"Shouldn't I put the luggage in the car?"

"What, and waste these bulging muscles?" She did an imitation of a body builder's pose. "I can handle it. Just do what you need to do. I'll pick you up the way we planned."

"You're the most incredible woman."

"And you are the luckiest man."

"Such modesty," I said, grinning.

"I love you, too. Now go. The sooner you get done, the sooner we can be together. I don't intend to spend my whole Christmas Eve alone."

I kissed her again, grabbed the smallest suitcase from the bed and let her lead me into the living room. I dared one more kiss then stepped out into the cold December night.

Tiny flakes of snow drifted lazily downward around me. Though I had shoveled our walk earlier, my feet crunch in the light coating that had fallen since. As I reached the sidewalk, I was overcome with the beauty of the place. Quaint little houses lined the three streets that made up the entire town. Simple candles and strings of colorful Christmas lights adorn nearly every home. The aroma of burning wood filled the air. The snowfall of the last couple of days was just in time to complete the traditional Christmas picture. The town was like a scene from a snow globe and could easily have been the model for the first.

I turned onto the sidewalk and strolled west toward River Road. I felt a sense of peace and completeness as I continued on to the end of town. My head was filled with happy thoughts and a deep thankfulness. It was hard to believe that just two years earlier my life had been about to end...

Chapter Two

The Chapel

I woke with a sharp pain in my thigh. The cardboard I had earlier pulled over me for protection against the wind was gone and the frigid wind stabbed easily through my ragged clothes. The policeman kicked me again, in the stomach this time.

"Move on, buddy. You can't stay here." His voice was callous and cracked with age.

I didn't argue, didn't even look up, just staggered to my feet and made my way out of the small alcove of the brick apartment building, back into the dark street. I knew I had to go at least a dozen blocks to be out of his beat. With luck, the next policeman would be younger and not so street-hardened. I longed to settle down and sleep in one spot for more than a few hours. How long had it been since I'd slept peacefully? A lifetime — no — two lifetimes... the lifetimes of my wife and little boy.

I gritted my teeth and trudged on, thankful there was no snow yet. Christmas lights glared at me from many of the apartment windows I passed. I didn't know for certain, but it seemed to me the dreaded holiday was only a week or so away. Just the thought of it gave me a sinking feeling inside.

I fought against it, but the memories of my last Christmas flooded my mind. I remembered the way Tabitha had laughed and joked until I broke the news. I remembered the way she had coddled Derek as I left the apartment that night. The accusation in her eyes had stayed with me every day since.

How could I have known? How could anyone have known that Santa Claus would be a jacked-up teen with an addiction in the apartment below ours? And who could have guessed that the kid would attempt to light a cigarette with his gas stove and instead catch his hair on fire? Like a campfire to kindling, the flames had spread rapidly through the dried wood of the old building. In just moments, all four stories had erupted into flames.

I rounded a corner and made my way east, my mind still toiling through the memories. I should have been there. I had desperately needed to be there. But once again my work had taken priority. "Another few months," I remembered telling her, "and we'll have all the time in the world. Another few months and we can move out of this apartment and get someplace nice for Derek."

"But we need you now," she countered. "It's Christmas Eve."

"I know, Tabby, but the partners are expecting me. We can still get a sitter if you want to go to the party with me."

"No!"

She hadn't been about to leave the baby alone on Christmas Eve. I might have been a heartless parent, but she wasn't. Ultimately, I had gone alone to the firm's Christmas party without her. I had left my family alone, instead choosing to be with a bunch of lawyers who neither thought about nor cared a single iota for me or for my family.

For those people and for my own warped sense of priorities, I had left my family alone to die.

In all, twelve tenants had been pulled from the building and laid with sheets over their bodies. Most, like my wife and son, had suffocated in the thick smoke. The police said Tabitha made it all the way to Derek's room, but there she collapsed. They found her beside the crib, her hand still grasping the lower rail. Neither she nor Derek had survived.

I was near the Holy Trinity Church when I finally shook the flashback. The biting wind didn't matter any more. I could never endure enough pain to wash my wife and son's blood from my hands. Even if I had been able to get a job and put my life back together, it just wouldn't be right. How could I continue in comfort in this world when the two most important people in my life now lay dead in their coffins?

I had been toying with the idea for months, and once again, thoughts of suicide ran through my head. Why should I enjoy the breaths that they could no longer take?

I wondered what had ever happened to the crack-head. Yes, he had survived the fire. Other than some singed hair he'd been fine. At first, I had hated him. I had even searched for him in a couple of halfway houses in the two months that followed the funerals. He wasn't at either place. The police told me they didn't know where he'd gone, but I suspected they really just didn't want me to know. It was my guess that the strung-out teen had followed his drug habit into the back seat of some drifter's van. He was probably lighting cigarettes with a gas stove hundreds of miles away.

It no longer mattered to me where he was. I ultimately knew who was to blame for the death of my family. And only a mirror could show me his guilt-ridden face.

As I approached the church, I once again wondered how I could manage to shoot myself. I didn't have a gun or the means to buy one. Money didn't come easy to the homeless, even those who were self-made.

Of course, I could have always called my father in Virginia and asked to borrow the money. I could have said I needed to buy a suit for job interviews. The fact that the old buzzard hadn't known or cared where I'd been in the last twenty years presented a bit of a problem. My last memory of him was his fist hitting the side of my forehead just before he threw me out his front door. No, asking him hadn't been an option, and even if it had, I would never have communicated with the monster. A wife-beater and a card shark were the kindest terms I could think of.

Though my mother had died when I was only six, I remembered her to be a wonderful and loving woman. But I also remembered her as a woman with bruises and lots of tears. After her death, my father had systematically beaten his next two wives who had both ultimately divorced him. He'd been pounding on a live-in girlfriend when, at fourteen years old, I had finally had enough. I stepped between him and the mousy woman and took one swing.

I've often wondered if I could have done more with my youthful anger, but I'd been so surprised by my solid jab to his eye that I hadn't thought in time to block his return punch. I had still been in shock as he launched me backward though the door, my hind-end slamming solidly onto the covered front porch of our house. I could still see the hatred on his face as the door slammed shut, and I remembered smiling at that last glimpse of his rapidly swelling eye. My single punch had been a good one.

I didn't have any other family, and I couldn't think of anyone else who would have helped with money. The twenty years since being thrown from my father's house had been filled with lots of hard work and schooling. Though I never borrowed a penny to pay for my six years of college, my round-the-clock work and school schedules hadn't left much time for socializing.

My only friends had been those I'd met at the law firm. And just how close we were became evident shortly after the double funeral. The first week brought me a large stack of cards and heaps of voiced sympathy, but by the second and third weeks I was struggling to stay ahead of the office innuendo that began to swirl all around me. I was making too many mistakes, missing large references in my legal briefs, not conversing well with clients and so on. Though some of the comments were partly true, most were just nonsense, voiced only to push me down and to make way for others to climb past me during my personal crisis. The way I saw it, the youngest lawyers, my 'closest' friends, all had begun to vie and scheme for my slightly larger office and my upcoming partnership position.

I didn't know if all the whispering and manipulation had any effect on my position at the firm or if it had been just a standard inquiry that brought me to the partners' notice. Whichever it was, just five weeks after the fire, I found myself sitting before all six of the senior partners, four men and two women. Not one of them offered a single condolence or even pretended to care about the loss of my family. The only issues discussed that day were the drop in the hours I'd billed out to clients in the last few weeks, and the problems I 'seemed' to be having with my written arguments. I remembered stuttering some vague excuses and assuring them that I would pull things together. I'd be back on track again soon.

I was on track, all right. Two days later, I quit. What was the use? I just couldn't bring myself to continue working with the hatefulness and deceit of the people around me. Besides, who really cared why one person was suing another? Did it really matter that someone's basketball had left black marks on their neighbors' fence, or that one woman's shed was built six inches too close to her back setback line?

I'd been relieved to get away from the entire pile of foolishness. But, there in front of the church, I knew those bridges had been burned. Whether by choice or happenstance, they just weren't there anymore. I had used up all my friends and close acquaintances with one simple tragedy—a tragedy that I had brought upon myself.

I tried to let the bitter memories go as I settled down into that sunken archway surrounding the church's main entrance. It seemed colder there than it had been at the apartment building, but by pushing back against the weathered bricks at the corner of the door I did manage to foil the worst of the wind. I had even imagined that a tiny bit of the heat from inside was seeping out through the edges of the door.

Thoughts of suicide had continued to churn through my head. I tried to remember every self-murder I'd ever heard about or seen on TV. For the longest time I concentrated on the problem. Finally, I decided that that throwing myself from the top of a building or in front of a truck would be the only options for me. God knew Albany offered many opportunities for both. I had come to this same conclusion many times before. Was it possible that I was finally ready to act on the thoughts?

I fell asleep for a time and failed to dream. When I woke, it was to a gentle hand on my shoulder.

"Come inside, my son." The priest's soft voice was accompanied by a warm smile that seemed to prove the sincerity of the offer. "You are cold and it's warm inside. Please come in."

He was a tall and good-looking man with gray hair and glasses. Though likely in his sixties or early seventies, his grip was strong as he helped me inside the building. As we walked through the main chapel, I couldn't take my eyes off the huge crucifix that hung over the dais. A separate light illuminated it nicely, though the rest of the lights in the large chamber were dim. Christ hung there, a crown of thorns surrounding his head, painted-on blood trickling down from the pricks in his forehead and the nails that went through his hands and feet. As large as he was, probably a little over six feet, and with all the detail of the sculpture, he looked convincingly real.

I might soon be sacrificed just like Him.

I immediately felt the sacrilege of the thought. There were no parallels here. Christ had died for something, in defense of the people he loved. I would be dying for no noble reason. I would be dying for my crimes, for my failure to protect my family, for my failure to shoulder the guilt and move on.

Again, as always, visions of Tabitha and little Derek came to my mind. Why couldn't it have been a pleasant picture of them full of happiness and life that haunted me? No, it was always the same, always the same image of them lying cold in their coffins.

"This way," the Priest said, drawing me from my reverie. We were at the base of the dais, and I realized I had been craning my neck to see Christ hanging some twenty feet above us. The blood was so real I imagined it would drip on me at any moment.

"He's still with us, you know."

I turned my attention to the kindly old priest. I nodded. "I suppose he is with you."

"With you, too," the priest said as he gently took my elbow and led me toward the small rooms that were his living quarters.

We entered into a medium-sized room, a combination kitchen-living area. There was a sink, a small refrigerator, a stove and some dark, wooden cabinets off to our right. A well-used couch and a wooden rocking chair backed up against the wall to our left. In the center of the room sat a chrome-edged table surrounded by three chrome and red chairs. There was no fourth chair, left out likely to allow more room to move around.

The doorway beside the refrigerator likely

led into a bathroom and the other arch, behind the kindly priest's rocking chair, was no doubt a bedroom entrance. There were a few prints of Jesus on the cream-colored walls, and one small, brass crucifix hung above the bedroom door, but otherwise the place was unadorned to the point of austere. I imagined that many priests probably lived with reasonable luxury. However, if those rooms were any indication, this one man's values were exactly where I suspected God wanted them to be; strictly and solely in the Lord.

Everything was immaculately cleaned, and I couldn't say exactly why, but I guessed the priest took care of that on his own. I suspected he would have been as comfortable scrubbing floors as giving sermons.

He patted my shoulder, and I didn't shy away as I would have with most people. "Family around here?"

"Not anymore," I answered. "My wife and son died."

"I'm sorry. The Lord sometimes can be a difficult master." He looked into my eyes and there was a genuine sympathy in his own.

"I don't blame him, God, I mean. I'm pretty sure he didn't have much to do with the dope-head who started the fire."

The priest nodded as he offered me one of the padded chrome chairs. He moved across the room and rummaged in a cabinet, pulling out a couple of mismatched cups. "Coffee?"

"Sure."

"You been on your own long?"

"If you mean homeless, not too long I guess. Only a few months, maybe six."

"You like it?"

"It's all I deserve. More than I deserve, really."

He scooped a teaspoon of instant coffee into both cups and poured water from an already warm pot into each. "You think it was your fault...them dying?"

"Why me, Father?"

"It's hard to know why God tests one and not the other."

"No, I mean why take me in like this? There must be dozens of homeless people all over the block."

He smiled, his eyes crinkling at the corners,

the right side of his lips turning up slightly more than the left, a kindly expression, somehow filled with wisdom and sympathy and understanding all at once. "You were the only one at the door tonight."

I couldn't help but laugh. I nodded. "You take people in every night?"

"No, most have learned to ignore my door. They don't come this way often."

"You torture the homeless?"

Again the slightly lopsided smile. He slid the black coffee across to me. "In a manner of speaking. Sometimes the right questions can be torture. Do you miss them?"

"No." I shook my head. Tears had somehow already formed in the corners of my eyes. Droplets began to course downward. "No, 'miss them' doesn't begin to describe it. Crave them. Need them so much my soul can barely stand the memory. That's more like it."

"And the guilt?"

"Nearly every minute of every day." I wiped my cheeks. "If I'd been there, I could have done something. I could have saved them."

"How do you know?"

"I don't. But by not being there I didn't even give them the chance."

"So it's all your fault?"

I shrugged. "From where I sit there just isn't anyone else to blame. I left my family alone on Christmas Eve, and now I don't have a family."

"Sugar? Cream?"

"No. Black is fine." I took a sip. It was bitter and warm.

"What next?"

"There is no next. I'm living better than I deserve, and I can't allow even that to go on much longer."

"You leaving us?"

"You know what I mean. I don't deserve anything."

The priest nodded, sipped at his own coffee, eyes half-closed, probably thanking God for the nourishment. He was the picture of contentment. I envied him. He looked at me then, really looked. His dark eyes, magnified by his glasses, were pools of both understanding and forgiveness. His was a gaze that children would long for and adults would seek. "What you don't deserve is the guilt. It wasn't your fault. There are invisible battle lines drawn all across our world. How could you have known your family was standing on one of them?"

"But it was my job to recognize there was a war, that there was danger. You can't just leave your family when there's danger."

The priest nodded. "I'm sorry, my son. It saddens me that you have been drawn into the horrible clutches of this guilt. I will pray for you."

"Thank you, Father—I'm sorry, I didn't catch your name?"

"Father Johnston, or Brian if you prefer."

"Thank you, Father Johnston. It was good to have been seen tonight." Not many people understood what it was like to be homeless. It was as close to invisibility as you could get. I really did enjoy being noticed. "I can let myself out." I took another sip and stood.

He immediately got to his feet and was

somehow taller this time. "You will sit and finish your coffee," he said firmly. There was no menace in his voice, but the tone was demanding, akin to the firmness of a parent to a teen-aged child. "We can have toast and eggs tonight, or in the morning when we wake. Either way, you will be sleeping in the warmth of the chapel this night."

I nodded.

"Now that you have been 'seen', there is no escaping my notice."

I could tell that this man understood the plight of the homeless. He was one of the very few who did. I slumped back into my seat and took another sip of the warm bitter beverage.

"If you'd like to take a shower, you're welcome to the bed." He pointed toward the doorway behind the rocker. "Or, if you prefer, the couch is fine just as you are."

Thoughts of Tabitha and Derek in their caskets came, as they often did, to my mind just then. "I don't feel like being clean right now, Father, if that's alright with you. The couch is fine."

He smiled again, warmth radiating from him as surely as from a flame-filled hearth. It was just unfortunate that I didn't deserve a reprieve from the cold.

I sipped again. The coffee was good.

Chapter Three

The Vagrant

The aroma of fresh-cooked eggs and toast greeted me as I woke. I lifted my head from the pillow and noted that a soft blue blanket had been placed over me sometime during the night. I almost hated getting up. The softness of the couch was a luxury I hadn't enjoyed in months. Father Johnston stood beside the table, that same kindly, skewed smile on his face. He was a doting man, and I couldn't imagine anyone not liking him. Had I intended to spend more time in this world, I would certainly have joined his Sunday flock. There was a cup in his hand.

"I'll leave this juice on the table. Your food is

ready, but you'll want to get to it before it's cold."

I stretched and sat up.

"I've duties to attend, but make yourself at home. Instant coffee's in the cupboard and the kettle should be warm for a while yet."

"Aren't you afraid I'll steal something and run?"

He humored me with one of those crooked smiles. "Everything here belongs to God, and you are a child of God. He happily shares with his children. Take anything you feel you need."

He placed the cup on the table and went out into the main chapel. As the door closed, I thought, *God has chosen his servant well in that man.*

I felt more rested than I had in days. It was the spiritual warmth of the place, I knew, that felt so comforting. How was it this environment had helped me make a decision that seemed the antithesis of warmth? The night before, I had finally made my mind up. I wouldn't go on living without my family. Not only did I miss them too much to breathe most of the time, I also knew I deserved no less than death. Today I would make final plans.

The eggs were scrambled just right and the toast was crisp with light butter,in short, perfect. Maybe it was because my own guilt had lifted somewhat, but the morning seemed brighter, cheerful almost. Finally I was going to take responsibility for my own actions. I was going to pay the price for what I had done. It felt right to know that my family would finally be avenged.

Even if the priest had been right in that my presence would not have saved Tabitha or Derek that Christmas Eve, I would at least be returning the score to zero. If I hadn't been able to save them, I too would have died in that fire. How could it be wrong to simply follow the plan God had originally laid out for me? I should have died that night, and only my greed and desire to get ahead in this world had saved me from that fate.

Maybe this visit had been just what I needed. Though it would likely have horrified him to know, I believe meeting Father Johnston had actually sealed my decision. I needed to kill myself. It just felt like the right thing to do. For the first time in nearly a year, I would be

taking control and doing something right. I
would not live through another Christmas without my family.

I finished up the meal and carefully brought
my plate and cup over to the small sink. There
was no sign of the priest's dirty dishes and I
felt as though I should wash mine and put them
away. I would have required a shower just to
be clean enough to wash dishes. With a twinge
of guilt I left them in the sink.

I made my way out into the chapel proper.
Father Johnston was beside the tall, wooden
dais. He was talking with another indigent-
looking fellow. The bedraggled man was nearly
as tall as the priest, in his forties, I would have
guessed by his face, though his dirty gray hair
suggested he might be older. His hair hung in
long curls well below his shoulders. I couldn't
say why exactly, but his long tangles looked
unnatural. I imagined that he might have tried
to braid his own hair and had the whole project
go sour. His tan trench coat was rumpled and
covered with dark and light spots that had long-
since rendered the original color a moot point.
What little bit of his plaid pants I could see

spoke of 1960s polyester, a thrift shop special not unlike my own, though my style sense had kept me in solid blue.

The hobo brushed a snarl of hair from his forehead and smiled over at me. I smiled back, consciously trying to remember if I had ever seen him in the shelters or kitchens. I felt certain that I hadn't.

"Thanks, for the meal and everything," I said to Father Johnston. "I really appreciate it."

"Is there anything else I can do for you, my son?"

"No, you've been wonderful and have helped more than you'll ever know."

"Come back anytime you like. You are always welcome under God's roof."

"Will do, Father."

I left then as the priest returned his attention to the other man. Strangely, the hobo watched me for a few seconds too long before turning back to the elderly patriarch. I wondered at his interest but couldn't quite place why it struck me as odd.

The wind whipped at my bare face and neck

as I crossed the short paved yard at the front of the chapel. I had some window shopping to do. Forming a plan shouldn't take long, but first I needed to be certain I knew all my options.

The rest of the day went quickly as I pushed my way through the throngs of last-minute holiday shoppers. I went from street to street, looking in the windows of nearly every pawnshop within walking distance. I even went into a couple of stores and managed to not be thrown out. I was almost ashamed at how pleasant the world suddenly seemed. It wasn't that I thought of Tabitha and Derek any less, it was just that I knew I would soon be paying for my crime. The guilt seemed to have subsided in anticipation of my upcoming punishment. Probably my new sense of purpose also helped, even if it was only to plan my own death.

I had already known firearms were likely out of the question, but while I was window-shopping anyway I confirmed what I already knew. Guns were expensive, even used ones. And now there were waiting periods when you bought one, not a viable option for me.

Stabbing myself didn't seem to be a good choice either. Though, admittedly, getting hold of a knife wouldn't have been too difficult. There were likely dozens of long and sharp ones at any of the three soup kitchens I frequented. As understaffed as they were, stealing a knife would have been a snap.

Unfortunately, I didn't think I could actually push a piece of steel into my own chest. And even if I could, the complications from missing a vital organ would be too great. I'd just wind up in an emergency room and then on to a psychiatric ward from there.

No, stabbing was definitely out.

I stopped in front of a pharmacy window. Crutches, Ace bandages and various other medical paraphernalia were displayed along with a three-foot plastic Santa and twelve plastic reindeer. There had been a time that Christmas brought a smile to my lips, but now the sight of the portly fellow in red just brought the grief back.

"Poison," I said through the window to the Santa as he reached plastic hands into his bag overflowing with plastic imaginary toys.

I needed to think this through. Would poison work? It might be simple. I could swallow a few well-chosen pills and that would be it. I especially liked the idea that I wouldn't be a shock to the poor innocent passerby who found me. To him or her, I would look only like a sleeping man down on his luck. Even upon discovering I was dead, they would have no horrible vision of death to carry around with them.

Unfortunately, self-poison involved the problems of both a lack of money and the possibility of the aforementioned emergency room journey.

No that was out, too.

Jumping in front of moving vehicles was next on the list. I leaned against the bricks of the pharmacy and stared into the busy street. I could easily have counted a thousand cars or trucks in just a few minutes. They sped this way and that, looking like hoards of colorful beetles intent on various insect missions.

I'd have to jump in front of something large and fast, like a bus, a truck or even a train. But what would happen to the driver who hit me?

I'd leave her or him with employment and legal issues, and maybe even a lifetime of guilt. Maybe I could leave a note in my pocket stating I had done it on purpose and that the driver had only the misfortune to have been there when it happened. But I imagined the horrific sight I'd have the bystanders remembering for years to come.

No, I'd never be able to do it. Cross another option off my mental chart.

I began walking the sidewalk again, moving silently though the shoppers who pushed by me, though all the while pretending not to notice me. Some days I would have gone out of my way to be noticed, to force them to see me, but today I was content to remain invisible and unnoticed in my lugubrious thoughts.

So what was I left with?

Maybe my commitment to suicide wasn't quite as strong as I'd thought. Was it possible that I was just making up excuses in order to shirk my responsibility? No more! Two wonderful people had died because of me. Was I forgetting my own implication in that tragedy?

Tabby's accusing glance from that Christmas Eve came back to me then. "You're really leaving us?" her eyes had said. 'Leaving us to die,' my mind finished for her.

No more excuses. I'd made the commitment to rid the world of my useless self, and I fully intended to follow through on it. My last option was to jump from someplace high. That was the way it would be. I would throw myself from a building or a bridge.

Of course, I immediately thought how horrible it would be for the people who found me. But there was obviously a downside to any method I chose. At least this was one I could afford and one that wouldn't leave anyone else feeling responsible. It was the best way, the only way really.

"Hey Buddy!" someone screamed. Suddenly, my collar was yanked backwards. Simultaneously, an explosion of sound and air erupted a mere foot from my face.

The train rocketed by like...well, like a train. I had been so deep in thought I'd nearly stepped right into its path. The thought brought a chuckle to my lips even as I fell backward into the shoulder of my savior.

My chuckle had become a raucous laugh by the time the man was able to pull me another few feet to complete safety. I stumbled and finally caught my own balance, but my laughter continued as the train rocketed past just three feet before me. There I had been, pondering suicide so deeply that I'd almost accomplished it by accident.

I was still laughing when the last car soared by and the world had quieted somewhat. I wiped the tears from my cheeks and turned to thank my protector, but all I saw were strangers. He was already gone. I hadn't gotten a good look at his face, but I knew it anyway. The plaid pants had been a dead giveaway. Apparently, the hobo from the chapel had been following me.

It took nearly an hour of darting up and down nearby streets to find him. The mottled stains of his trench coat finally came into view just three streets from the chapel. Was he reporting back to the priest about me? What had I done that morning of any interest to anyone?

Nothing, I hadn't even done anything of interest to me.

"Hey you," I called out. A red Volkswagon bug, one of the new ones, swerved around a corner and sent me scurrying back up onto the sidewalk. "Hey!"

He stopped and slowly turned toward me, brushing the snarls of his gray hair away from his face.

Four lanes of busy traffic divided us. I pressed the crosswalk button, but knew it could take as many as five minutes before it was safe to cross.

"Wait up! I want to talk!"

His head nodded, and I couldn't help but feel that this was exactly the way he had planned it. Had he wanted me to follow him? Was anyone really smart enough to plan something like this in advance?

Oh sure, I thought to myself, *and he probably made me nearly walk into that moving train, too.*

It seemed an awfully long time before the green hand flashed. Finally, I was able to cross.

He was more handsome than I would have

thought from the brief glance I'd gotten earlier. My guess at his age had likely been right, though, somewhere in his late-forties. As I got within a few feet of him, the mystery of his too symmetrical snarls became apparent. It wasn't really hair. He was wearing a wig that looked similar in quality to costumes I'd seen kids wearing on Halloween.

He must have caught the direction of my gaze, because he laughed and pulled the faux-hair from his head. Beneath was a neatly cut, full white crop of hair. He was looking less-and-less the part of a vagabond.

"Thanks for the help back there," I said.

His face broke into a smile filled with good white teeth, and it seemed to be genuine. Much like Father Johnston, this man was immediately likeable to me, but in his case I couldn't say why exactly. It was just a feeling I got.

"How come you were– "

He never let me finish the sentence. "I followed you."

"Why?" I was truly perplexed. A need for caution crept into my mind. Kind or not, this fellow's actions seemed increasingly bizarre.

He stared down at his feet. My eyes followed. His brown leather dress shoes were older but in fairly good condition with a decent sheen. They were quite different from the torn sneakers that I now wore, tape holding the sole of the toe onto the right one. I'd have to re-tape it soon as it looked as though all my walking today had nearly worn through the bottom of the duct tape strap. In truth I hadn't really been homeless long enough to have worn a pair of shoes through like this, but I had been broke enough to sell my own shoes a few months back. These sneakers I'd picked up at a shelter the same day.

He was staring at me when I looked into his face again. "I'm new at this…this homeless thing," he said. "You seemed like someone who might be willing to help."

"Help you what, be homeless? Not much to it really. Live outside, sleep outside, get ig-nored a lot. That pretty much covers it." I con-sciously smiled so he'd know I wasn't making light of him.

He gave me his big-teeth smile again, and this one was filled with full-fledged cheer.

What followed was a bear-deep and infectious laugh. I couldn't help myself and broke into a cheerful fit of my own, a laugh that Tabby used to say was akin to the squawk of a goose. For several moments we stomped feet and continued caterwauling, likely looking to the rest of the world like a couple of drunks or psychotics or both.

I hadn't felt this buoyed in a very long time, and it definitely was the man beside me that elicited the response. My joke hadn't been all that funny. I knew I could easily have been friends with this man had times been different.

As our laughter subsided there on the sidewalk, he held his stomach as if too physically stop his rumbling. The sight gave me a clue to something that had been nagging at me since first seeing him at the chapel. It was like Santa's laugh, minus sixty or eighty pounds.

"It's a Santa wig," I said pointing at the poor excuse for dreadlocks he held in his hand.

He nodded. "'Found it. I mixed in a lot of dirt to get the color. Thought I'd fit in better than with a new haircut out here." He waved toward the city in general.

"So eyes have been following you with the fancy shoes and nice hair?"

"Exactly."

"Sorry, but I'm not going to be of much help. I'm tied up at the moment."

"Busy day walking into trains and such?"

The statement didn't sound quite sarcastic. Had he guessed at my plans for the future, or more specifically my lack of a future? Could the priest have said something to him? Didn't seem likely.

"Thanks for the help back there. I'd have been a mess without it."

"No problem. We all need help sometimes." He pointed at himself and gestured toward his clothing in general. "Case in point." He put the ridiculous wig back on.

I had to admit he did look less of a mark with it in place. I nodded my approval. He might not get a date, but it would keep the muggers away. "You need help finding the shelters, food-kitchens? What exactly?"

"I'm hoping you can tell me how to survive? How do you manage from day to day? Don't the homeless just pop up dead everywhere?"

I tried to determine if there was a hidden message in his last statement, but there was none I could discern. "You just keep on plugging everyday. Don't trust anybody, and don't sleep anyplace where it's too comfortable."

"Too comfortable?"

"Yeah. Ever notice how the police are constantly shooing our kind from one doorway to the next, from one alleyway to another? There are dozens, hundreds of places you could sleep where there would never be a policeman: under the bridges, down some of the abandoned subways, inside vacant buildings and so on. We don't go there, though, not those of us who still claim any value in our lives."

"Why not?"

"Only two kinds of people can survive in those warrens."

"Two?"

"Yeah, the gangsters and the goners."

"Goners?"

"Those are the people who don't care if they

live or die. Some of them might even prefer the latter."

He grinned wide again. "Did you just say 'the latter'? Never thought I'd hear a word like that coming out of a homeless mouth."

"Sorry. I was a lawyer once. Though I've learned to tone it down, the useless words crop back up every once in a while."

"So if I don't care if I survive I'm safe in those other places?"

"No, it's just that if a goner dies it's no big deal, not to them, not to anyone. They might live a day, a week, a month or even a long lifetime in one of those forgotten holes, but when their number comes up, they're gone. It's a risk that most of us just aren't willing to take."

And, I thought, *it's not guaranteed so doesn't work into my suicide plan.*

"Any other words of wisdom?"

"Yeah, don't be homeless. Go back to your life."

He smiled again, and this time I sensed a secret hiding in his dark, glimmering eyes. But the unspoken mystery disappeared as his eyes lowered and his cheeks drooped. "I had a life, a pretty good one," he said, "but I made some really stupid decisions and—well, it's all gone now."

"You don't have a pension, money to live on?"

There was no smile this time. He eyes had gone from brown to a lighter shade of hazel. His words were slow and seemed to be chosen carefully. "I have no option but to be here right now."

I accepted that, knowing full well there were chapters unspoken. I had apparently touched on a sore point. Everyone had secrets and sins of some kind. What did it matter to me? I'd be gone soon.

"Were you heading back to the church?"

"I thought the Father would know where I could eat."

"I doubt he'd tell you. He'll more likely feed you right there, his own lunch if that's all he has."

The filthy Santa wig bounced in agreement. "He is a good one. You can see it in his eyes."

I nodded. I wanted to say something more but realized I didn't even know this man's name. It's funny, because as a homeless person you learn never to give out your name and to never ask each other about them. Names made it too easy for family to track you and too hard to avoid the constant street crime investigations. Detectives roamed the rough neighborhoods almost as often as those of us who lived there. The only names we usually used were handles and nicknames that tended to be changed often and at whim.

"I'm Skip," I said, revealing my real name for the first time in at least a couple of months. I wasn't sure why, but it seemed important to me that this man knew it. Maybe I was subconsciously trying to be remembered by someone, if only by another poor soul like myself. "Why don't we get something to eat? Martha Big's is only a few blocks this way." I pointed north, toward the industrial park.

"That a restaurant?"

I laughed. "In a manner of speaking, I suppose it is. Let's go."

The afternoon on Albany streets can be deceiving. The buildings were just high enough that the sun, which had really not yet begun to set, looked lower in the sky than it really was. It was only two o'clock as we strolled north toward the food kitchen, but the shadows along the sides of the busy highway were long and growing dark. As we passed from busy street to busy street, the shadows became islands of darkness, spaced in exact rhythm to the height of the buildings on our left. Along the way, I learned his name was Barwood Stone, and that not even he knew how such an odd name had been chosen for him. He'd apparently grown up in an orphanage and never had the chance to ask his parents about his decidedly offbeat moniker. His life had been spent scheduling freight shipments on the northern leg of the Boston and Maine Railroad. The job had ended a number of years before, just phased out, much the way railroads in general had been disappearing for years. He had no children, and though he hinted at having been married he never actually came out and said it.

Our discussion had grown silent for the last half-block or so. It was my turn to share some personal history, and I was surprised at how difficult it was to begin that verbal journey.

Strangely, it wasn't the tragedy of the fire that was so difficult to talk about, it was more that I couldn't seem to mentally get through it to the lifetime I'd had before. I was both perplexed and shocked. I couldn't believe I hadn't realized this sooner, but it had been months since I'd recollected anything about Tabby or Derek from before that Christmas Eve. It was almost as if their deaths had erected a barrier, separating the homeless Skip of today from the working-two-jobs law school student and budding lawyer Skip of my earlier life. The revelation was like a wash of ice cold water down my back. I shivered with realization.

We now stood before Martha Big's kitchen. Thankful for the excuse, I opened the sagging green door for Barwood and waited a full thirty seconds until I followed him in. It was funny how life was. I couldn't bring myself to talk about my pre-fire past, and now I suddenly knew why. I was afraid that if I remembered any of the good things I might lose the courage to pay for my crime. It was easy to think about the loss of my family, the loss of my job, and even the loss of my self-respect as I

joined the street world, because those thoughts
fueled my personal disgust and sealed my desire to be done with this life. Those other
memories, though, those good things that had
happened were much too dangerous to recall.

Was I really such a coward that I couldn't
face life and leave it at the same time? I didn't
give myself time to consider the answer
because I was already following dirty Santa
locks into the dim, basement-level kitchen that
we all knew as Martha Big's.

She wasn't especially tall but was about as
large a woman as I'd ever encountered, likely
topping four hundred pounds. Her weight,
though, most of the homeless soon discovered,
didn't slow her down even the slightest. She
moved back and forth through the throngs of
indigent people and directed her dozen
volunteers like a general on a battlefield. One
minute she'd be cleaning up a dropped tray at
one end of the large, low-ceilinged room, and
the next she'd be directing a young girl on how
to scoop a fair portion of food into every plate.
Every few minutes, she'd disappear into the

cooking areas that were off-limits to us, and I had no doubt she was just as busy back there directing volunteers on matters of cooking importance. No, her size was very secondary to her energy and to her heart.

We got our food and found seats near one wall that afforded a pretty good view of the entryway and most of the dining hall. We might have seen the entire room from here if it hadn't been for the spindly Christmas tree that had been erected about two-thirds of the way down our wall. One of the long tables had been placed at an angle to make room for it. The lighted star was only an inch or so from the low, open-beam ceiling.

"That's Martha," I said, pointing subtly at the force of nature that moved about the ragtag groups of seated men and women. Almost as if she had sensed our attention, she looked our way and smiled. It was only the briefest of glances before she continued about her business.

To his credit, Barwood never said a word about her size. Instead he said, "She works hard, doesn't she."

"Like a whirlwind. The old-timers say she used to be homeless herself, but somehow pulled herself out of the streets. A few years later she was back, but this time to help."

"You sound like you admire her."

"Who wouldn't? I don't think I'd have the character to do what she does—obviously don't because I'm here not there."

"You could be running this place," Barwood said.

I wanted to say something smart, like 'yeah, you're one to talk,' but I knew where he was coming from. For the first month or two on the streets it was hard to get used to your own failure. It was almost as if you were the only guy on the streets with a clue. And you felt the need to tell others how they could better themselves. Soon, though, Barwood would come to realize that he needed to worry about himself and getting his own life together. Besides, for me it didn't much matter. My life had reached its pinnacle long ago. Things had been heading downhill for quite some time, and I had nowhere but further down to go.

We finished the meal of fried-potatoes,

hotdogs and peas mixed with onions. It was all reasonably good. I was ready to leave but detected that Barwood wanted a few more minutes to talk. I'd spent this much time with the guy, so what were a few more minutes? My plans could wait that long. I had decided, however, that any discussion of my own past was off limits. Now that I knew why I had avoided the subject earlier, I knew there was no sense in making what I had to do any harder. I would pay for the crime, but I wouldn't beat myself with memories beforehand.

We made our way though the busy cafeteria and refilled our coffee mugs before returning to the table. I saw Martha glance our way. Normally, she asked that diners move back out into the street when they were done with their meal. I knew she didn't mind us being there, it was just that there were only a hundred or so seats, and with several hundred people to feed each meal she had to keep the turnover steady. She must have realized that Barwood was new and that he needed some time, because she nodded silently at me as he and I settled back down in our seats.

"I was going to kill myself," Barwood said.

Here it comes I thought. *Father Johnston did set me up.*

"Why didn't you?" I responded half-heartedly. The second this turned into a lecture, I was prepared to leave.

He shrugged. "Things came up."

I waited but he added nothing to the statement, no long discussions about the value of life or pleadings for me to not do this. Barwood just sat there, a muted sad droop to his face.

He apparently really hadn't known, because if he had, it was the oddest lecture I'd ever received. I decided to wait him out in silence, make sure I'd seen all the cards before getting any deeper into the discussion.

"I left Maine to do it," he continued after some time. "Took a bus to Vermont."

"Why Vermont?"

"Heard a rumor about a place called Christmas Leap where lots of people killed themselves. I figured with no I.D. on me, they'd never know who I was and my ex-wife would never find out."

"Where is your ex-wife?"

"In a hospital in Portland—Maine, not Oregon. She's in the psyche ward. Tried to kill me...almost did. I have a pretty good sense of taste and could tell she'd mixed something in the brandy. I pretended to drink it but really dumped it in the sink. I didn't realize she had spiked her own, too. She downed two full glasses before I figured it out. I called for an ambulance. She's been at the hospital ever since."

"Why'd she do it?"

"Women and gambling, mostly."

"Yours, I assume."

That brought his great and wonderful laugh back. He nodded in the midst of the guffaw. "Yeah, the women were mine. And I don't think she ever gambled more than a dollar at a time."

"How long ago?"

His cheerfulness ended abruptly. I'd touched on a sore point again. Finally, his face calm and voice measured, he said, "Doesn't matter much."

"How'd you get from Vermont to Albany?"

"A friend."

I knew for certain there was something unspoken in his story, some large block of logic that I was missing. I was equally certain that he intended it that way. There was more to this white-haired man than plaid pants and a dirty Santa wig, but as I had determined earlier it made little difference to me. I had a course to follow that had nothing to do with Barwood or his Swiss-hole past.

"So what's this Christmas Leap thing about?"

He looked at me then. There was a depth to his stare that was a little spooky. "There's a town called Gray, up to the north of Vermont, near the Canadian border. It's just a bitty place, few houses, couple of stores, and a fast river that runs past. The river comes out of the mountains so fast that it has cut a gorge at least a hundred feet deep. A bridge crosses over it right near town. The locals call it Christmas Leap."

"So people commit suicide there?"

He nodded. "River's fast and deep. The locals say one goes over every year, like clockwork."

"On Christmas?"

"Christmas Eve, actually."

"Obviously, you didn't."

"Like I said, things came up but the attraction was there. It seemed a clean way to go, and I imagined if you had to do it, why not be part of a tradition."

"Doesn't the town keep police there?"

"Town doesn't have any police. They're so far up that it sometimes takes an hour just to get one of the sheriffs out their way."

"Sounds horrible," I said, but I was fascinated. It could be the plan I'd been looking for. Barwood stared at me, that faint smile still playing on his lips.

He no doubt expected my story then, the story that I had determined was not going to be told. I guzzled the rest of my coffee. It was just hot enough to burn as it went down. "You might want to go back to the chapel," I said to him as I got abruptly to my feet. "I'm sure Father Johnston will let you sleep there tonight. And tomorrow you should go back to Maine. Go back to your life. Trust me, the homeless outdoors thing just ain't much fun."

He stood, his face a neutral mask. I sensed

there were oceans of unspoken secrets in his eyes. I didn't care to know any of them. There was a little town in Vermont waiting for me, and his secrets wouldn't make one bit of difference to what I had to do.

"Thanks again, Barwood. It was nice meeting you. And good luck."

He extended a hand. It was clean and soft, not at all like the coarse palm one expected to find out on the streets. This man did not belong, and I hoped he would heed my advice and go back home.

"Good luck to you, Skip."

"And you," I said as I turned and left. I could feel his secretive eyes boring into me as I wove my way through the crowds to the door. I followed a smelly, young woman out into the open air. It made me sad to think I would never eat there again.

"Good luck to you, Barwood," I whispered as I pulled my collar tight around my neck and went in search of a calendar and a map.

Chapter Four

Preparations

There were three newsstands along Main Street, and I felt certain I could find everything I needed at any one of them. I reached into my pocket to see how much money I had left. There, I discovered only two very wrinkled ones (my emergency money) and about thirty-seven cents in change.

The date was easy. A quick glance at any one of the many newspapers declared it was December twenty-second. I had only two days to find my way to this Christmas Leap. Now I just needed to know where Gray was.

"Do you have a map of Vermont?" I asked the grizzled old man who crouched closely beside his news cart. The crouch might have been to ward off the wind, which was especially biting that late-afternoon, but I suspected it a spinal issue.

"Don't got map."

I didn't recognize his accent, but his attitude was all too familiar. He was really saying, *Get out of here, you bum. You're driving away the paying customers.* I was in no mood to create a scene, but neither did I intend to leave until I found out what I needed to know. My eyes darted up and down the full racks. "What are those?" I asked, pointing to a row of what looked suspiciously like road maps.

The man uncurled his upper back with obvious effort. He was actually six inches taller than I would have guessed, which made him easily four inches taller than my five-foot, ten-inch frame. "No maps. I told you."

Knowing that I'd likely get the same response from each of the other two newsstand owners, I opted to press on. "Those *are* maps," I said evenly, "and I want to know how much they cost." I stared hard into the grizzled eyes. They were growing narrower by the second.

He glared for a moment longer but then nodded curtly. He'd obviously decided that I wasn't going away that easily. "Five dollar. You have? If no, no waste time."

"I have two," I said showing the crumpled bills.

Eyes narrowed again. The man's back must have been growing sore because he was sinking back down to my height. "I sorry. I can no take two." His response wasn't as rude as before.

"Can I just SEE a Vermont map for two dollars?"

The man studied me through bushy brows. Like a wilting flower, his back had arched all the way back down. His eyes were now an inch below my own. "You travel to family?"

I didn't want to lie but knew the wrong answer might ruin whatever chance I had. "I'm traveling for Christmas. I need to be in Gray, Vermont by Christmas Eve."

He relented and I held out my two dollars. In an amazingly quick movement, his wrinkled hand snatched away the bills while his other grabbed the right map off the rack and held it out to me. I felt as though I'd just witnessed a magic trick. Money disappears as map appears. He might have been a pickpocket in an earlier life.

"No rip," he said.

I unfolded about half of it and was quickly able to locate the town in question. Vermont wasn't a large state and the towns were clearly indicated. Just as Barwood had said, it was right up near the Canadian border.

That night passed as slowly as any I could remember. I was cold and miserable, and my few short naps were interrupted both by police warnings and my own thoughts about a certain bridge in Vermont. In all, I moved five separate times before dawn arrived. And, by the time the sun was climbing over the Albany skyline, I was already wandering nervously throughout the city.

I couldn't explain it exactly, but I was drawn to this Christmas Leap as surely as a magnet was drawn to steel. On the one-year anniversary of Tabitha and Derek's deaths, I intended to pay for my crime. It seemed like an eternity, but finally I began to notice store front gates opening and shopkeepers going in to begin their day. The Greyhound station would likely be open already.

Clots of fog formed from my breath as I strolled toward the bus depot. Vermont State Highway Fifty-seven went right past the town of Gray. I never had been one for mass transit, but it seemed reasonable to think that one of the bus routes would go somewhere along that highway. If I could get close enough, I could hitchhike or even walk the rest of the way.

I lost my train of thought as I noticed a number of Christmas wreaths that hung haphazardly from the evergreens that lined the concrete walkway in front of the Greyhound station. A quick glance to the building beyond suggested that they had been above the windows until just recently. Only about half the wreaths still hung in place. Wire hangers and bits of greenery suggested spots where the other wreaths had originally belonged. Strings of Christmas lights from the roofline had been torn down and were hanging like forest vines all across the face of the building. A heavyset man in a gray jumpsuit stood on the walk out front and spoke rapidly into a cell phone as he stared angrily up at the decorations that had been torn asunder. I imagined him to be the depot manager or possibly the person in charge of building maintenance. He was no doubt calling in an electrical crew and ladders.

The gray brick exterior of the station looked like many Albany inner city landmarks. It was covered with spray-painted graffiti of all types. From the look of the security guard who wiped frantically with a rag at some of the most of-fensive comments, the artwork was a recent addition to the station. Every few seconds the guard would dip his rag in a can I assumed to contain paint thinner. A police cruiser sat in the parking lot to the right of me. Inside, I could see an officer jotting notes on a clipboard.

It was probably a good thing I hadn't tried to sleep near the station last night. The thought had crossed my mind, but I feared it was a little too close to gang turf. The condition of the building proved my assumption to be true. It must have taken a crew of eight or more kids to do this much damage in a single night. As I walked past I felt bad for the guard. It would take him all day to clean even a portion of the spray-painted scrawl, and from the angry grimace on his face he knew it.

Inside the depot, the floors were concrete and surprisingly clean in comparison to the mess outside. Though I didn't imagine the ticket counters had been open last night, I thought all bus depots were open to passengers twenty-four hours a day. The graffiti gang had obviously not come in, so the doors must have been locked. Though it looked clean, I could smell the cloying scent of cigarettes and body odor. This could be a very hectic place at times, I surmised. There were wooden benches lining the outside walls and sets of back to back benches were placed every few feet along the center of the floor.

I could see by the large white clock on the wall that it was just a few minutes after eight when I walked up to the only open service window. A pretty brunette woman who appeared to be in her early thirties sat there. She looked me up and down and nodded tightly.

I couldn't say why, but my appearance never seemed to bother me until I came in contact with women near my own age. It wasn't embarrassment for attraction reasons, I didn't think. It was more because I was always reminded of my wife. Standing before that young woman, I felt as though Tabitha was seeing through her eyes and was appalled by what she saw.

"Can I help you?" The ticket attendant was straightforward, but not rude.

"I don't have money for the ticket right now," I told her, deciding to be truthful from the start, "but I will get the money before I come back."

Her look softened somewhat. I was glad I hadn't made up some bogus story. "I need to get to Gray, Vermont," I said. "Do you have buses that go that way?"

"We go every which way," she answered. She punched a few keys on the computer. "If Gray is spelled like it sounds, we have a stop right there in town."

"How much would it be for a one-way ticket? And when is the last bus that could get me there before Christmas Eve?"

"Christmas Eve is tomorrow, sir."

"I know. I really need to get there." I felt

the tears pooling at the corners of my eyes. It surprised me how important this had become. Two days before, I had been drifting aimlessly around the streets of Albany, and today I had a goal that burned so brightly it made me cry to think I might fail. I had to get there. I would not let my family down again. I wiped my eyes, embarrassed. "How much time do I have to raise the money?"

"Let's check," she said, her voice sympathetic. "Can I get you a pen and paper to write this down?"

"I can remember," I said. "Not much else on my mind right now."

She smiled warmly. "You'd have to be back here by nine tonight. We have only one bus that could connect you that far north on time. One way would be seventy-five dollars."

I felt as though I had just been punched. Seventy-five dollars! There was no way possible I could raise seventy-five dollars in a week, forget in single day. The best beggars I knew didn't make that kind of money. And I wasn't exactly in the attorney profession anymore.

She must have seen the defeat on my face because she said, "I can do better than that." She punched several more keys and a machine gave out a high-pitched whizzing sound.

"Here you go. I have the authority to give a thirty-three percent discount for customers who have a legitimate complaint. The high price seems like a legitimate enough complaint to me. Just hand fifty dollars and this ticket to the teller when you come back tonight."

I dumbly took the ticket. I had learned over the last few months that the homeless don't often see kindness from normal people. We're invisible, and when not invisible we're a source of shame. My eyes began tearing again as my fingers closed around the paper.

"Open one more time," she said.

When I did open my hand again, she inserted a bill. "It's the best I can do. I've got two kids, and their dad doesn't pay support like he should." She closed my hand again with her own. "I hope it helps. Good luck."

"Thank you very much," I said. "Really...thank you."

I turned away then, not so much for my own

benefit as for hers. I could see her own tears beginning to form. "Merry Christmas," she said loudly enough for me to hear as I passed through the front doors to the outside walk.

Chapter Five

The Challenge

I walked several blocks before I looked into my palm and saw the ten-dollar bill. Forty more to go. I knew from past experience that begging was a slow and arduous process. I had panhandled only twice before, but each all-day stint had netted me less than the teller's sole gift. It just wasn't realistic to think I could reach my goal that way.

I ambled down the next alley and waded through the first dumpster I came to. I found only one bottle, and even that had the label torn off. Though I wasn't sure if the store would take it, I stuffed it inside my jacket anyway.

The second dumpster gave a better haul. I found a vinyl bag and two returnable cans. I stuffed my three nickles into the bag and re-thought this particular action. Even if I could manage to come up with enough bottles, by the time evening came around, I would look and smell so bad that no driver would ever let me on the bus.

There had to be another way.

While I was thinking through the possibilities, I went through several more dumpsters. I had the best luck in one belonging to a steak restaurant. There, I found twenty-eight beer bottles. All in all I came up with one hundred and sixty-three bottles by mid-day. Combined with the money from the ticket attendant that morning, my total net was up to eighteen dollars and fifteen cents. I was still short thirty-one dollars and eighty-five cents.

I gave up then because I had already de-cided on a new course of action. On the way to Jenny's variety, I honed my plan. Admittedly, there wasn't much to hone because I intended to speak with the same blunt honesty that I had used with the ticket attendant.

I walked the three blocks to Jenny's. She

was there behind the counter when I walked in with my vinyl carrier and other trash bag, both full of cans and bottles. Her muscular arms were folded and there were lines of disapproval in her forehead.

"You steal them bottles from some poor kid?"

"You know me better than that, Jenny," I said dramatically. "I wouldn't do that."

"Not 'less you had the chance."

"No, really," I said. "I got these fair and square. Well over a dozen dumpsters worth to be exact."

Jenny was a homely blond woman in her fifties, and she was built more like a rugged male contractor than any woman I'd ever met. She'd been known to drag full-grown men right out of her store and into the street, and none had ever been foolish enough to fight back. This street-wise gal was used to every manner of con conceived. Though I wasn't a normal offender, she gave me the same go-a-round everyone else got. Her raised right eyebrow and squinted left eye seemed to say, 'I know you're lying to me,' and, 'spit it out before I throw you out'.

"I need to get some money together," I told her, amazed at how guilty her stare could make me feel. I hadn't done anything wrong.

"Drinkin' again?" she asked. She didn't cater to alcoholics, at least no more than she legally had to. For instance, she could insist that I wash each container before she accepted it.

"No," I said. "I haven't had a drink in over four months. I never was an alcoholic."

"That's what the worst of 'em say."

"It's true, Jenny. I need the money because I'm leaving the city."

"Oh?" She pulled the bag to her side of the counter. One at a time she started removing the cans and bottles and placing them in a shopping cart beside the cash register. The cart seemed ridiculous in a store this small. I'd have been surprised if it could fit down even two of her four narrow aisles.

"Life ain't any easier in Syracuse or Rochester, you know."

"I wouldn't imagine it would be," I said. "I'm going to Vermont."

"Family?"

"No."

"Friends?"

"Nope."

"How many you got?"

"You're not counting?" I asked.

"You know how many there are. Why do it all over again. How many you got?"

"One hundred and sixty-three."

"Eight dollars and fifteen cents it is then." Listening to her talk, it was easy to believe Jenny wasn't overly bright, but the way she came up with a total so quickly illustrated that there was more to her than one might first think. She punched several keys on the register and the drawer spit open with a ringing clang. As she passed the money to me, she said, "They don't put up with your kind in small towns, you know. Wouldn't surprise me if there isn't a single person living out of doors in the whole state of Vermont."

"I wasn't planning on 'living' there."

The look of curiosity was still on her face

when I thanked her and left. If I knew Jenny, she'd start asking everyone on the block what I was up to the second I disappeared around the corner. Of course, no one would know. Within hours there'd be more rumors about my plans than there were people living on the whole street. I might even become a legend. Imagine, Skip Ralstat urban legend, the homeless man who split town and made millions in Vermont cheese or who inherited a billion dollars from his great, great-something-or-other and ran off to take over the family mansion.

A half-hour later, I was still smiling at the imaginary life I would be leading when I came to Capitol Square. I contemplated whether it would be better to go straight into the Governor's office, or into one of the community welfare buildings. Ultimately, I decided to try the Governor's office, only because it was the easiest to spot. Gold domes aren't all that common.

I was surprised that there was no guard to direct me as I entered through the swinging glass doors. Even though governors were fifty times more common than our President, their positions should at least warrant a clerical person at the door to question visitors. Even Wal-Mart had greeters.

The foyer was simply a wide hallway with dozens of oak doors opening off to either side. About a hundred feet down the hall, a circular stairway rose beside four elevator doors. In the center of the hallway was a three-sided kiosk. I read through the directory and couldn't find a single reference to the Governor.

I'd heard the state was cutting back, but this was getting ridiculous. Thinking there must be more names, I moved to the next side. This second directory did have more names, but they were under the heading of *Building Two*. I checked, just to be certain. He wasn't mentioned there either.

The third side of the kiosk solved the mystery. It was a diagram of Capitol Square, which consisted of a series of parks and public buildings. An arrow indicated that I was actually in a building adjacent to but not quite connected to the Capitol Building. The Capitol's front entrance would be ninety degrees to the east.

The hall was filled with bustling people

whose eyes darted purposefully away whenever I looked in their direction. Sometimes I
forgot I was had become member of America's
lowest class, the homeless, but being intently
ignored by so many people at once sparked a
tiny bit of anger in my chest. Weren't people
all the same, regardless of how much they
made or where they lived?

I wanted to say *yes*, but I knew better.

Since I was already in the building, I scanned
the directory and decided to visit the
Department of Health and Human Services.
From my few brushes with State Assistance
cases at the law firm, I suspected they might
be able to help. I could always move onto the
Governor's building if I had no success.

On another day, I might have enjoyed riding
the elevator, if for no other reason than to make
the other passengers squirm and stare at their
feet for the duration of the ride, but today I
had more important things to do. I had only
four or five hours left before these offices
would close, and I didn't know how many bu-
reaucrats I'd have to visit before I'd be suc-
cessful. I took the stairs.

Office 220 was on the second floor, about the tenth door down on the right. I had to squint to read the brass plaque on the door. This was the place. I considered knocking, but suspected it was proper to just walk in.

A trim, middle-aged women of Asian decent sat at a desk in front of me. Her fingers were resting lightly on the keys of an electric typewriter, a dinosaur in this age of computers. The woman's large almond eyes stared at me, but she hadn't yet said anything. The silence was uncomfortable.

"Yes?" she finally said. "What can I do for you?" Her voice was firm and authoritative. In those seven words, I could tell this was not a secretary. I had happened upon someone in charge with my first try. I hoped it was a good omen.

"I need your help."

Her eyes glided evenly down then back up my torso. Whether what she saw pleased or displeased her, I couldn't tell. Her expression remained passive and professional.

"Yes?"

"I'm not quite sure how to begin."

"Please, sir, I don't mean to be rude, and I hope you won't take it that way, but my secretary is out and I have at least two dozen calls to make. I also hope to have this report finished and in the Governor's hands by the day's end. I think it would be quicker if you would explain your problem to me."

"I live here in Albany and I'm homeless."

Though I suspected the homeless were not her concern, she didn't break in to tell me that. She simply nodded and waited for me to go on.

"I want to leave the state tonight, but it's fifty dollars for the bus ticket. I only have eight dollars and fifteen cents, and I'm hoping the city or the state will give me enough for my ticket and maybe for a few meals when I reach Vermont. I will be happily on my way, and the city will have one less homeless person to be concerned about." I knew I could have said more, but honesty tends to be brief and to the point.

The woman continued to look at me with her large brown eyes. They were beautiful. There was an unusual intensity about her. It was as if she gathered her energy for long periods so she could then burst forth, no holds barred.

"Okay," she finally said.

"Okay?"

"Yes, okay. I will help you, but only if you'll promise me something."

"Such as?"

"I want you to promise to try your best to stop living on the streets."

"I promise," I said. I'm sure she didn't mean for me to 'stop living' entirely, but I was being truthful.

She went to a closet at the back of the office and came back with a small gray pocketbook. She opened it and withdrew a black leather purse.

"I didn't mean for you—"

She looked sharply up at me. "Whether it's from me or from the state, the money all comes from the same place. I'll just be paying a little higher percentage this way."

"I didn't mean to beg."

"Didn't you? Isn't that what asking the government for help is? If people like you would stop acting as though the world owes you a life, it would be a much more pleasant place."

She held out four bills, all twenties. I stared at them for a long time. I wanted them, needed them to get to Vermont. The bills seemed to swell then shrink before me.

"No, thanks," I finally said. "I don't want your money. Not for your reasons, anyway. It's people like you that create this dependency. You can't belittle a person in one breath and then expect them to grow self-respect and self-reliance with the next."

I left her then, her beautiful eyes wide, her mouth agape. I closed the door firmly behind me.

"How stupid," I mumbled to myself as I trudged back down the stairs. Without ticket fare I couldn't get to Vermont.

I knew it was my own stubborn pride, but accepting that money would have been wrong. It would have been an insult to the memory of my deceased wife and son. Though possibly the biggest mistake I'd made in a long time, it felt good to take a stance. I hadn't exactly been the picture of citizenship lately.

I imagine the crowds still ignored me on the way out but, to tell you the truth, I was so wrapped up in my own thoughts that I didn't even notice. Once outside, I turned west, away from the Capitol building. The idea of visiting the Governor's office no longer appealed to me.

I guessed it was around one o'clock when I crossed through the last clump of trees that would take me out of Capitol Square. That meant I had only eight hours to raise the needed money. The question was "how?"

If I continued to think of this journey as a dedication to Tabitha and Derek, that also meant the way I got the money would be as important as the journey itself. I had to find a more wholesome way to finance my trip.

Somehow, I had to work for it.

Jenny was hunkered over the counter, as she always was, when I returned to the store. Adam Walston was counting out pennies in front of her. There was a bottle of Coors sitting between them.

"I'm only eight cents short," Adam said. He wiped his dripping red nose with the greasy sleeve of his parka. The green hood was down and his wild brown hair was more tangled than usual. He could not have put his hands through that mess if he'd tried.

"Ain't that close enough, Jenny?" he pleaded.

"Not for beer it ain't," the big woman said. She whisked the full bottle up into her sizable paw and placed it in the shopping cart she had used earlier for my returnables. "Now for food, or juice, or even a package of cookies, I'd let it slide, but not for beer. Never."

"I need it," Adam said. His eyes were fixed on the cart.

"That's the end of that discussion," Jenny told him. "Now get out. I wish you'd buy that junk from someone else anyway."

"You're the only one that helps us," Adam said. "We all come here."

"Why don't you buy some food instead? I'll sell you any food in the store at half-price."

Adam's shoulders slumped and his eyes fell to the floor.

"Lord's sakes, all right! I'll get you a beer, a cheaper beer. Just stop your belly aching."

Knowing a good thing when he saw it, Adam
nodded but remained silent. Jenny picked up
the bottle in the carriage and carried it out back
to the coolers. She returned with an unlabeled
bottle that had a dark amber beer in it. "Here,"
she said, putting the bottle down on the
counter. "It's brewed by a friend of mine, but
it's good stuff. Now go get a box of donuts and
give me your eighty-eight cents."

Adam wiped his sleeve across his nose again
then went and did as told. Anxious to get back
to his beer, he grabbed the first box of donuts
he came to. I imagined they would soon become
pigeon food, that is if he didn't throw them
straight into the trash.

I waited patiently as he counted his money
a second time. Before Jenny could pick up the
first coin, he grabbed his groceries and
disappeared out the door.

She stopped and watched him through the
window as he rounded the corner of the next
block. There was such a look of tenderness on
her face that I wondered if there might be a
connection between them.

"Relative?" I asked.

"Nah, just another one of you guys. Did you know he's only twenty-two? Just a baby."

"Why'd you give in like that?"

"Ain't no beer in there," she said with a chuckle. "A swallow of apple juice will do him good. The trick only works once, but once is better than nothing. Say, what are you doing back here?" she asked. "I figured you'd be on your way to the mountains by now."

"A woman offered to give me the money I needed for the ticket," I said. "But I turned her down."

"I gotta hear this one." Jenny leaned over, her stern chin resting on her hands, thick elbows braced on the counter.

I told Jenny exactly how it happened and why I hadn't wanted to accept. She politely listened but I could see the mirth building inside her. As the last word left my lips, she let loose a great bellow of laughter.

"It wasn't all that funny," I said sourly.

"I just can't imagine you playing the righteous role."

I nodded. I hadn't shown a lot of backbone during my acquaintance with her. And she hadn't known me before...well, just before. "Believe it or not, I used to be a good guy. Not the best maybe but pretty good. This last year, though, it really took the wind out of me. I guess I just stopped believing in people. Mostly, I stopped believing in myself."

"You really going to Vermont?"

"Yeah, I really am. For the first time in a long time, I know I'm doing the right thing."

"I'll give you the money," she said.

"Thank you for the offer. You've helped all of us so much. I often wonder why. Why cater to the poorest people in the neighborhood? Half the time we don't have money. We drive the better customers away. And most of us are either drunk, or nasty and often we're both. Why would you do that?"

Jenny stared up toward the rust-spotted tin ceiling above. She had that same look she'd given Adam a few minutes before. She reached out and took my hand.

"I do it because it's the right thing. I do it because it makes me feel a little better about taking so long to come east in search of my father. I do it...because I want to."

"Your dad?"

Jenny closed her eyes and shook her head. She squeezed my hand, and I think I understood. I, too, found it difficult to talk about Tabby and Derek. Even though I thought about them all the time, I felt violated when other people asked. It was as if I didn't want to share them with anyone else.

"Tell me what you need," Jenny said.

"A job for the afternoon that pays at least thirty-one dollars and eighty-five cents."

"What if I said fifty?"

"I'd say I want to earn all fifty."

Within minutes, she had a broom in my hand. She led me out into a huge back storeroom. It was easily four or five times the size of her store. In it were fifteen rows of metal shelves filled with canned and dried goods. There would be enough here to feed an entire building of tenants for weeks.

"Why?" I asked.

"Just a little dream of mine," she said. "I hope to open a shelter here next year. The food is cheap when you buy it in bulk, so whenever I have a few extra dollars I stock up. I've also got an apartment upstairs filled with sheets, blankets and towels. The only thing left to buy is the furniture."

"You own the building?"

"Three of them actually. About forty-seven apartments in all."

"Where?"

"Right here, side by side. When I get number ten-ninety-seven at auction next spring, I'll own the whole block. That's when I'll start the shelter."

I had a dozen more questions, but just then the store bell rang. She had a customer, or maybe Adam had come back to complain. She left and I set to work. I had swept out the storeroom and was about ready to begin on the back loading area when Jenny rushed back in.

"Adam's been shot!" Her lips quivered as she spoke. "You've got to get over to Cagney's and find out what's going on. Come back as soon as you know."

I hurried out.

Cagney's Liquor Store was really a front for the gambling business that three teen drug dealers had started up a few years before. The store was five blocks north of Jenny's Variety. I ran all five.

By the time I wheezed up onto the sidewalk, the police had already cordoned off the area. I moved through the crowd to see what I could. The store's picture window had been shattered. Glass shards littered the area. An ambulance was backed up onto the sidewalk, and I could see two medics kneeling over a victim in the back of the emergency vehicle.

I scanned the faces of the cops but didn't see any that I recognized. How was I going to find out anything? Not only was I concerned for Adam, I was also Jenny's employee right now. Getting information was the task she had given me.

"Excuse me," I said, stepping boldly over the yellow plastic ribbon.

Immediately, two policewomen converged on me.

"Move on," one of them said. "This is a crime scene." She heard that line on a TV drama, I thought.

"If he's Adam Walston," I said. "I can tell you where to find his parents."

"We can locate the family without you," the policewoman informed me.

"I doubt that. They're homeless."

The two looked at each other then back at me. "Where are they?"

"I'm a friend. I'll tell you, but only if I can find out his condition and what happened."

"We can't do that."

"Do I look like CNN to you? I'm not going to say anything. And even if I do, who'd believe you ever actually told me."

The two women glanced to each other. There was a long hesitation. They knew that crimes involving the homeless often became unsolved John Doe cases. I imagined the paperwork and effort in trying to identify these people could be tremendous. Finally, there was a mutual nod. The tallest one turned to look at me. "The boy's hurt...badly. He broke the window and was trying to steal some booze. I can't say how, but someone shot him before he got any. Now your part, where are his parents?"

"In a cemetery near Greenwich," I said. "He told me they died in an apartment fire. He ran away from his foster parents about eight years ago."

"That's not much help," the shorter one said.

"I didn't say it would help. I just told you I knew where they were."

"Did he have other family?"

"None I ever heard him mention."

"Get out of here, then."

One woman held the yellow plastic ribbon up while the other ushered me beneath it. I stayed a few minutes longer and watched the medics work. It didn't take a genius to figure out he was dead or close to it. Why else wouldn't the van have been on its way to the hospital by now?

Jenny's eyes were red, but she was no longer crying when I got back to the store. I hesitated in telling her what had happened. I knew how she would interpret this.

"Dead?" Jenny asked.

It was painful to see the apprehension in her face. She really didn't want to know.

"I think so," I said. "The police were cagey about it, but it didn't look good from where I stood."

"It was the liquor store?"

"Yeah. Looks like one of those gorillas shot him after he broke the big window."

Jenny shook her head. She was fighting back the tears. "I should have just given him the beer."

"If it hadn't happened today, it would have happened tomorrow or the day after," I told her.

"Did I tell you he was only twenty-two?"

"I know."

"I should be alone," Jenny said.

"I'll watch the store if you want."

She shook her head. "It's all right. Won't hurt nothing to close the doors for a little while. You're money's in here." She held an envelope out to me.

"Wait," I said. "I haven't earned—"

"Shhsshh! I'm the boss around here. I know what you've earned and what you haven't. And I don't want you to look in there until you get to the bus station. Okay?"

I nodded.

"Good." She released her grip on the money.

"I also want you to grab a couple of sodas and some food. And if you don't do it right now, I've got a mind to sweep this floor with your head."

I smiled as her attempt to be her normal self, and I did as told. I picked a softdrink and a box of Pop-Tarts™.

"Are you going to the hospital?" I asked.

"Yeah, someone should be there."

"And if he's dead?"

"Then I'll make the arrangements. The system may have forced that boy onto the streets, but it sure ain't going to store him in a public urn."

"His parents were buried somewhere near Greenwich."

"Maybe," she said. "I know that's what he told everyone. Wouldn't surprise me, though, to find they're living and breathing somewhere."

"You might want to check near Greenwich anyway."

"I will. I promise I will. Have a good trip."

"Thanks for everything," I said as she let

me out. The store's interior lights were already off and she had drawn the shade over the locked door.

"Skip," Jenny said through the partially closed door.

"Yeah."

"I've always been sorry about what happened to your wife and son."

I nodded. "Me, too."

Chapter Six

Hidden Saints

I wondered if there was something more I could have said to help Jenny through the guilt she was feeling. It did occur to me how ironic that thought was. Who was I to be doling out guidance or support? God knew I hadn't been much of a shepherd over my family or myself.

It was late afternoon and the temperature was already beginning to fall as I made my way back to the bus depot. A city worker stood about twelve feet up on a ladder and was checking the Christmas lights on one of the large lighted bells that hung high from one of the sidewalk light posts. "Should that cord be unplugged?" I asked, pointing to the wire that dangled about eight feet above my head. The man looked over at it and down at me. He chuckled.

"Thanks, buddy," he said. "I unplugged it to fix the harness and for the life of me have been able to figure why it wouldn't come back on."

"Glad I could help."

"Thanks again."

"You're welcome." I continued on past. I was shivering now. If the cold of the last few nights had been any indication, the mercury would hit in the single digits here in Albany tonight. Thankfully, I would be sleeping in a warm bus and not on a cold doorstep. Come to think of it, I would never have to sleep in the cold again. Suddenly, doubt filled my mind. Was I doing the right thing? Maybe I should sleep in the cold every night right up until I'm one hundred years old. Was I taking the easy way out?

I smiled grimly. I knew I was trying to talk myself out of this again. It wouldn't work, though. I intended to follow through. Soon I'd be in Gray Vermont and I'd do what had to be done.

The bus station looked much neater than it had earlier. The spray paint was all gone, and the broken strings of Christmas Lights had been hung back up around the eaves of the roof. Even the colorful Christmas wreaths over the windows had been returned to their proper positions. It surprised me how the cheerful decoration brought a smile to my lips.

It was just four o'clock when I walked through the double swinging front doors into the lobby. It had been only eight hours since I'd been here last, and I was five hours early for my bus. At least there was no chance I'd miss it. I walked up to the service window. The woman from earlier was gone. A man sat there, instead. He was wearing a red Santa cap with a white pompom on the end. It was completely out of place atop his gaunt face. Too thin for a Santa and much too stern for an elf, he had angular cheeks and a chin that jutted out like jagged sculpture. He stared at me with thin lips and narrow eyes. I easily imagined his face hadn't seen a smile in months, maybe years.

"Hi," I said and handed him the discount ticket.

He looked at it and then me with skepticism. "This discount was for you?"

"Yes."

"And your complaint was regarding...?" His question drifted off as his eyebrow raised at me.

"I have no intention of getting into that again," I said forcefully. I didn't want to get the woman from this morning in trouble, and I desperately needed him to accept the discount offer. Without it, I wouldn't have enough money for the ticket. At least, I didn't think so. I hadn't actually opened Jenny's envelope yet. "Do you intend to help or not?"

His eyebrow fell. "You don't have to be rude."

"No? Your company didn't offer to replace my lost clothes, did it? Nor my wallet?" I allowed my voice to rise. "You think these last three days have been fun?"

I paused, gauging the reaction I was having

on him. The narrow eyes had disappeared and his thin lips had smoothed out. "We lost your luggage, sir?"

Up until now I had been careful not to lie. His assumptions had filled in the blanks from my comments. "I told you at the beginning I'm not getting into this again? Do I need to call your main office?"

"No. No. Not at all, Mr—," He glanced down at the discount ticket, "Mr. Ralstat." He shook his head fervently. "There's no need at all. I'm very sorry for everything." The gaunt man's left eye had begun to twitch and his voice trembled.

I felt bad. "It's alright. The discount has been a help." I pointed at the ticket.

"Can I do something more for you on the price?" He was almost begging.

"No. I'm fine, thank you. The first discount will be fine." I opened the envelope. As I'd imagined, Jenny had given me more than I needed. I handed him her fifty dollars.

"Very well, Mr. Ralstat." A few computer keys were pushed and a quivering hand passed me the ticket.

"Thanks," I said. "It's not everyone that would have asked about my trouble."

He visibly relaxed and gave me the first smile I'd seen from him. It suited him, melting some of his harsh angles. I smiled back.

I turned and glanced to the paper Santa mounted on one of the concrete block walls. The cheerful old legend seemed to be grinning at me. I winked at the likeness. It would be our secret.

I took a seat at a bench that overlooked the busy thoroughfare in front of the station. Vehicles of every conceivable size whizzed to-and-fro in a frenetic dance that almost seemed to make sense, but not quite. I thought of my wife and son and as the time passed was surprised that happy images of them came freely to me. I spent the next few hours reliving moments from the wonderful year we'd spent together. Even though we'd been married almost two years before Derek was born, it seemed that Tabby's and my love for each other, already strong, had grown a hundred-fold upon his birth. Even though I had worked a lot during that year, we spent many magical evenings and weekends together. They were like two angels who graced me with their time and their love. Visions of park playgrounds, the museum and even long drives along the ocean came back to me. I could feel the cool ocean breeze whipping at my hair while Tabby and the baby goo-gooed to each other from the front and back seats.

I remembered, too, some of the little things, like the time Derek had learned to first fling his food with a spoon. That first heap of mashed potatoes had landed squarely in the center of my forehead. Though maybe I should have scolded him, I simply laughed and flung the gob right back. Before another bite was taken, we had all three been reduced to toddler-style food-fighters, each one more covered with dinner than the next. We were forced to eat toast later that night, Tabby determining that Derek and I weren't as likely to begin flinging solid foods at each other. As it was, the little bumpkin did smear a bit of butter on my cheek as he climbed into my lap. I fought my urge to smear him back, but at some point a Dad had to be the example. So, I simply hid his toast on my head instead.

When the memories began to fade, my cheeks were streaked with tears of happiness at having spent time with those two magical people again. I had missed them so much and couldn't believe that months had passed since I'd remembered any of those things.

I wiped the tears and looked about me. I found that nearly five hours had passed. It was a few minutes to nine and the station was filled with crowds of people. I'd been so involved with my reminiscence I hadn't noticed the building filling up. Though every seat was taken and dozens were forced to remain standing, no one had opted to sit on the bench beside me. Such was the life of the homeless, or maybe it was simply the life of the unwashed. I knew I qualified on both counts.

I used my last fifteen minutes of wait time to pull a strawberry Pop-Tarts™ free from its box. Though not the height of modern cuisine, it was good and filled the hole that had formed in my gut.

A woman's voice announced that the Albany to Montpelier bus was now boarding. As I got up and made my way to the gate, people were moving aside to let me pass. I estimated that at least twenty people in the waiting room had stood and were holding their bags. Yet, they all let me pass even though this was their bus, too.

I suddenly became aware of my unshaven face and dirty bedraggled clothes. Something about getting on a bus with people seemed more intimate than passing them on the street or brushing against them in a hallway.

I handed the gate attendant my ticket and hurried out the door and up into the Greyhound. There were a dozen passengers already on the bus, most towards the back. Even with the twenty or so people I'd seen getting ready inside, it would not be a crowded trip.

Ignoring the snort of an elderly woman near the door, I made my way about halfway down to the left before taking a seat. No one sat within two seats of my spot. Those same seats would probably stay empty all the way to

Vermont. I'd have the next best thing to a private trip.

As the other passengers boarded, I could see many concealed glances my way. And, just as I had expected, the seats around me stayed clear. My privacy would be guaranteed unless the bus became so full that incoming passengers would be forced to sit closer.

Back when I had a life, I always drove or flew to wherever I wanted to go. As a consequence, this was the first time I had ever experienced the tortoise like, stop and go progress of a Greyhound. It seemed to take hours just to get out of New York, and the old saying about a bus trip being a never-ending journey became clear as every stop brought new passengers just as it disgorged others.

I only had to change buses three times on my way to Gray, and on that last connection I managed to get the back seat. For most of the ride it was dark outside, so I didn't see much of the countryside. It was the Christmas season, however, and decorative lights were sprinkled throughout every large and small community along the way.

I watched those lights with pangs of regret. Though I knew I was doing the right thing, my mind seemed to be latching onto the little pleasures and using them against me. I didn't sleep, couldn't have.

Chapter Seven

The Santa Shop

When I finally stepped off the last bus, it was late morning on the day before Christmas. Christmas Eve was just hours away. The air here was cool, and my breath came out in great chilled clouds that I half-expected to fall to the ground as ice. I tugged my collar up as close to my ears as possible and thrust my hands in my pockets. The bus roared and began to pull away from the curb. I imagined a great,unified sigh of relief had just occurred on that bus. The vagabond was gone.

There was no actual bus depot here, just a little sidewalk sign that read, *Bus Stop, Gray.* A green wood and steel bench sat directly beneath the sign. Though the sidewalk had been

well plowed, two or more feet of snow had
already fallen here. A single bank of clean white
snow lined either side of the road. It was tiny
and quaint village just as Barwood had
described it. There couldn't have been more
than fifty buildings comprising the entire
community. Tall evergreens rose against the
backdrop of the roofs in every direction.   It
was as though a tiny village had been carved
out of the northern wilderness which I
supposed, in fact, it had been.

Fortunately for me, the sky was clear and
bright and the town had plowed both the streets
and the sidewalks. I would be able to move
about easily.

To find the bridge first was probably the
best idea. What a lark that would be, to come
all the way to Vermont for a suicide only to
get lost and never find the bridge. Though Gray
was just a tiny village, that was no guarantee
the bridge would be nearby. It was conceivable
the bridge was miles from the township proper.
The bus might even have passed it without me
noticing. I hadn't realized we were this close
to town until the driver had slowed for the Gray

stop. I hadn't seen a soul out of doors yet, but was tempted to make my way into one of the small shops that lined the short street and ask where the bridge was. Of course, that would have been like out-and-out saying, 'I've come to be the next victim of your Christmas Leap.'

No, unfortunately, I would have to find this bridge on my own. I took out another Pop-Tarts™ and munched as I crossed the street. Immediately opposite the bus stop was a little store painted a brilliant red with white trim. Atop the roof was the largest Santa hat I had ever seen. Constructed of plywood, it was mounted and painted in the same bright colors as the house. I think it would have been tacky if it hadn't been for the time of year and the snow all around. As it was, it seemed perfect.

Just below the hat, near the roofline, hung a sign declaring the building to be *THE SANTA SHOP*. I could see an amazing assortment of toys in the window and for curiosity's sake I opted to go inside. Maybe I could find a way to casually ask about the bridge while I was there.

An aggressive wind chime clattered as I

opened the single wooden door. The smell of fresh sawdust and paint assailed my nostrils as I ambled into the simple but strangely appealing showroom. Wooden toys were placed in neat rows along carpeted shelves that lined every foot of the long room. The toys were wonderfully bright, seeming to come in every conceivable color. I didn't think I had ever seen so many hues and color variations in one place at one time. As I looked closer, I realized that these were not the typical wooden 'crafty' toys you would usually see at flea markets and discount shops. No, these were works of art that just happened to be in the form of toys. There were smiling dolls, jointed lions, leaping tigers, and colorful animals of every type. I could see cars and trucks from every era, and Victorian carriages pulled by finely carved wooden horses. There were wooden buildings, enough to build entire cities, and tiny jointed people that had been hand-carved with such impeccable detail that I almost expected them to up and move about.

I ogled shelf after shelf filled with spectacular playthings of every type, and I did it with a childish awe I knew I hadn't felt since I was a young boy. About three-quarters of the way down the large room, on the third shelf up I saw a blue wooden truck that sat beside a series of bulkier tractors. My breath caught. I knew that truck. I think I even believed that if I picked it up I would find a tiny version of me and my father sitting in there, waiting for the sun to rise so we could fish. It was one of the few childhood memories of him that I could cherish, and I think that's what made the truck doubly attractive to me. I wanted so badly to pick it up that my childish yearning made me queasy inside.

"Go ahead," a deep friendly voice said to me. "Try it. The wheels turn and both doors open. It's a good little truck."

I pulled my gaze from the toy and looked to the man who had just come through a door at the back of the store. From the strengthened wood scent and the sprinkling of sawdust on his flannel sleeves, I surmised he made these toys.

"It's good to meet you," the man said, striding forward and extending a hand out. He was shorter and thinner than his deep voice would seem to indicate. I was immediately reminded of Barwood and was struck by this man's forthright sincerity. His smile was infectious and I readily returned it.

"Nice to meet you, too," I said, taking his strong hand in my own.

"Here," he said. He lifted the truck gently from the shelf and placed it in my hand. "We glued steel bearings in all four wheels. It's quiet and rolls fast."

I stared at the little blue pickup and it was like being transported back to that morning beside the lake. It was a time when my father and I were not enemies. He was dressed casually, unlike the suits he usually wore. He tousled my hair and talked to me about getting the biggest fish ever. I listened with awe and was convinced we'd catch a monster fish so large we'd have to chain it to the truck just to get it home. He was just a dad taking his son fishing, and I was just a loving son enjoying every minute of the attention. I'd almost forgotten that I had loved him once. And this memory almost convinced me that at one time he had even loved me back.

I shook my head and gazed at the pickup truck. Though only five inches long and less than two inches high, it was the most incredible toy I'd ever held in my hand. I could sense a quality about it that I knew only the most expensive collectible toys could hope to emulate. Most modern toys were plastic or die-cast metal, stamped out in the thousands or even the millions. They lacked personality, I thought, and craftsmanship. This little truck, however, had both. Though it was made of wood, I couldn't see a sand mark in it. And the paint was flawless, shining as brightly as any Matchbox I'd ever seen. I spun one of the front wheels. True to the shopkeeper's description, the wooden tire whirled effortlessly.

"It's wonderful," I said. "You make these?"

"That, and everything else you see here." He gestured proudly to all the toys on the shelves.

"I was really just browsing. I saw the Santa hat on the roof and was just curious what your store was like."

"Oh, we love browsers," he said. "It's nice

to have our work appreciated."

"You own the store?"

He stared off to the left for a minute, then smiled and nodded. "Yeah, I guess I do. I officially take over tomorrow."

"You bought this place?"

"Heck no. My boss gave it to me."

"Free and clear?"

"Yeah, it's mine. Gave me his house, too."

"And a house?"

"Sort of a Christmas present."

"Your boss sounds like an unusual man." I didn't know whether I thought he was truly generous or just crazy.

"He's the best man I've ever known," the toy maker agreed. "Sorry he's not here for you to meet. You'd like him."

"You been working here long?"

"Only a year now. But he's taught me an awful lot in a year."

A year, I thought. Who gives away a store and a house to someone you've only worked with for a year? This man must have been family to the owner.

"Well, congratulations on the store, and

thanks for showing this to me." I tried to hand the truck back to him.

He shook his head. "No. You keep it. That truck belongs to you. I could tell just from the way you looked at it. Toys and people are like that, you know. Some just belong together."

"I'm not connected to a toy," I said, but the words felt like a lie as they came out of my mouth. "And I'm about the last person in the world that needs one."

"You don't understand," the man said gently. "It's free. It's my Christmas gift to you."

Strangely, I was furious. Money wasn't the issue. As a matter of fact, Jenny had given me over fifteen more dollars than I had needed for the bus. I knew my thoughts were irrational, but I felt as though I was being scammed. I thrust the truck harshly back at him. "I don't want it," I said. "I just don't want it."

The man's smile never faded, growing instead somehow softer with understanding. "I'm sorry. I can see I was bothering you," he said. He accepted the truck and placed it gingerly back on the shelf.

"I should have been finishing up my projects

instead of coming out here to rudely interrupt
you like I did. You make yourself at home and
just holler if I can help with anything."

He shook my hand a second time.

"If I don't see you again before tomorrow,
have a great Christmas." He turned and strode
back out into the workshop. I couldn't detect
even a hint of insincerity in his voice or manner.

I looked around the shop again, but the
initial magic I'd felt was gone. And I knew it
was my fault. It was as though I'd just
committed a sin in church. Filled with guilt, I
walked back out into the snowy day.

I made my way to the restaurant two stores
down from The Santa Shop. Glumly, I trudged
inside and settled down at a bench near the door.
There were only three other customers I could
see, two elderly women sitting at a table near
the back and one middle-aged man in a black
snowsuit. He sat at the long counter that ran
the length of the room. There was a cooking
area behind the counter where a large balding
man in a blue and white striped shirt worked
silently stirring and turning various bits of

food on a grill. He didn't look up to notice me. There were a dozen empty tables and at least that many empty bar stools. For the owner's sake, I hoped business was more brisk during regular meal times.

A heavyset brunette waitress dressed in the same striped blue and white uniform as the cook hurried over to help me. I could see the smile noticeably drop from her face as she got a good look at me. It's also possible that my aroma was stronger than she was used to.

"What can I get you?" she said tersely.

This was the type of treatment I was used to. I felt all the more guilty for the way I had treated the Santa Shop keeper that had gone so far out of his way to be nice to me.

"I'd like two slices of toast, orange juice, and a bowl of Frosted Flakes™ if you've got it."

"We don't have cereal."

"Pancakes?"

"Blueberry or regular?"

"Regular is fine."

She was eyeing my chest as though I had a third arm sprouting from it. I looked down to see the Pop-Tarts™ flap hanging out of my jacket breast. Embarrassed, I pulled the box out and laid it on the table.

"I bought it for the bus trip," I said, feeling like an oaf. "Forgot it was in there."

For a long moment, she stared at me with an I-know-you-stole-it-and-I-hope-you-have-money-to-pay-for-this-meal expression. I was happy when she scribbled a few notes on her pad and left me to my own.

Right about then, I was tempted to grab my Pop-Tarts™ and take the door. However, that would have proved her theory of me and, besides, I deserved a last meal. Better to stick around and show her that I actually did have the money to pay.

Regardless of the stiff service, the food turned out to be wonderful. Martha Big did her best as did the other shelters, but compared to that this food was pure ambrosia. I was wiping my toast across the last of the syrup in my plate when the waitress returned. She laid a bill beside my empty glass.

"Will that be cash or charge?"

I'm not sure exactly why her attitude had

angered so much. Maybe I just wanted to get in a few last licks before the cold river took me. Or maybe I was just born to be crude. Either way, I leapt to my feet and stared down at the rude little woman.

"You're not a very nice person," I told her. "And if you are, you're not a very nice person to me.

"I'm happy for you if you have a warm place to sleep every night, and I'm happy if you don't have to wonder when and if you'll get your next meal. That's great for you. But is it too much to ask that you have a little courtesy? Is it too much to ask that you treat me like a human being?"

The stern look never left her face. "Will that be cash or charge?"

Drained of the fight, I said, "Cash," and handed her a ten.

"Merry Christmas," she snarled as she came back and slapped several bills and a handful of change on the table. She took two steps back and seemed to be waiting for me to leave.

Like a bouncer, I thought. I could see that the other three customers were trying not to be conspicuous but they couldn't help but stare. I didn't blame them. The cook hadn't glanced my way even once during my visit, but just then I caught his eye. He shrugged and shook his head as if to say, *Doesn't matter. She just doesn't get it.*

"Yeah, Merry Christmas to you, too," I said to her as I stuffed the Pop-Tarts™ back into my jacket and the change into my pocket. Then I thought better of it. I pulled out the one-dollar bills and laid them on the table. What use did I have for the money, anyway?

The woman's eyes flickered from my face to the money and back again. She shook her head. I could see the struggle of emotion in her face.

"That ain't right," she said. She picked up the bills and held them out to me. "I don't deserve a tip."

"You fed me didn't you? That's more than some restaurants can say."

She nodded. "I'm sorry, sir."

"Don't sweat it. Apology accepted." I buttoned my jacket and left.

I wondered at what had just occurred. Somehow a bad encounter had turned good, all because I decided to leave a tip in spite of my own anger. There was a lesson to be learned here. I was only sorry that I wouldn't have a chance to make use of the knowledge...then again, maybe I would.

I strolled purposefully back to The Santa Shop. Once again, chimes sounded off as I entered. Bright colors and cheerful wooden faces greeted me. I grinned as my eyes lit upon the little blue truck on the third shelf up.

"Excuse me," I said loudly, but careful not to holler.

The friendly man instantly emerged from his workshop in the back. His face was bright with a smile. There didn't seem to be any falseness to him.

"I'm glad you stopped back," he said. "What can I do for you?"

"I wanted to say I'm sorry for acting the way I did."

"It's all right, really. It's a shame, but Christmas is a difficult time for a lot of people.

I'm fortunate that I found the spirit again. Or, more correctly, I should say the spirit found me." He grinned widely.

"Must be easy to have the spirit when you're surrounded by all this." I gestured toward the bright shelves.

He surveyed his little store and seemed like a proud father, standing over his children. "You're right. The Christmas spirit is strong here."

"It must be nice to watch the children."

"Yes, it is. But we're all children, you know. We bigger folk try our best to be brave and strong. But inside we're all just kids. Sometimes seeing the sparkle of an adult's eyes over the right toy is even better than seeing that of a child. Children are surrounded with the magic of life, but so many of us forget all about it as we get older. I know I did."

"Me, too," I said.

The man nodded at the truck. "I sure wish I could convince you to accept the truck. There's a lot of pleasure in giving, you know. You'd be doing me a favor."

"In that case, I accept."

"Good." He crossed the floor in three easy strides. With reverence, he lifted the truck from the carpeted shelf again and handed it to me.

"Merry Christmas, little boy," he said, his smile as wide and genuine as one can be. "Merry Christmas to you."

I could think of no words to match the emotions that threatened to overwhelm me. "Thank you," I said simply as I took my present and left.

"No. Thank you," I heard his voice amid the ringing chimes. Then the door closed behind me.

Chapter Eight

A Last Hurrah

The bridge turned out to be only a twenty-minute walk from town. It was also surprisingly easy to find once I noticed a street sign declaring *River Road*. Though brief, the walk to the river was scenic. The town of Gray sat on a plateau that separated a series of four mountains in the east from a deep gorge and another cluster of mountains in the west. River Road skirted along the edge of the town's plateau and offered a breathtaking view of the snow-covered gorge and the western mountains beyond. Sheer granite faces dotted the otherwise white peaks in the distance. Painted against a brilliant backdrop of blue sky, the scene was like a picture you might find on a puzzle.

As it happened, the bridge was one of those tall, black steel affairs. Barely two cars wide and at least a hundred feet long, the charcoal structure extended from the edge of the plateau, across a deep ravine, all the way to a ridge on the other side. I peered over the edge and gasped. It was easily a hundred feet straight down to the soupy mixture of ice and black water at the base of the ravine.

No wonder people killed themselves here. It was certain that no one could survive the fall.

I backed away from the edge and waited for my heart to return to normal. There was an irony here, I knew. It seemed ludicrous that I was ready to leap from the bridge, but the chance of slipping and falling from it terrified me.

I walked a little further back toward town and leaned against a tree, comfortably distant from the edge of the ravine. For a while, I watched the water and ice churn slowly downstream. The wind was biting. My breath emerged in great clouds, and even with my hands stuffed securely into the depths of my woolen pockets I could feel them stiffening in response to the frigid Vermont air.

If I wanted to survive long enough to leap tonight, it was obvious that I had to get back to town and find a warm place to hole up. The thought of a movie theater was a pleasant fantasy, but Gray didn't look big enough to even have a video store.

During the walk back, a man in a silver Cadillac™ crossed the bridge and stopped to offer me a ride. I caught the look of derision as he eyed me up and down and could see relief on his puffy face when I declined.

"Merry Christmas," I whispered as he gunned the engine. As if in response to my sarcasm, the Cadillac's™ big tires spun snow up into my face.

Unlike the Albany station, Gray's bus stop was nothing more than a sign and a bench. There weren't even a few rectangles of Plexiglas™ to break the wind. I thought of cuddling up on the open bench, but it would surely be too cold and would bring suspicious eyes my way.

There was no other restaurant along the

small strip that I could see, but there was an old Victorian home with a sign out front that identified it as *Andy and Sue's Bed and Breakfast.* I went inside.

I realized immediately that I should have knocked but against my expectations the front door deposited me right into the living room of the large Victorian House. There was no hotel desk and no bell to ring. Fortunately, the large room with plush furniture was empty. I hadn't interrupted a TV show or other gathering.

"Hello," I said in a loud voice.

"Hi. How are you?" A handsome thirty-something man strode casually into the room. He didn't act at all surprised by my presence and didn't perform the same scathing eye exam that I was generally used to.

"We were just preparing dinner. You're welcome to join us if you're hungry," he said. "Or, if you like, I could show you to your room?"

The man was so open and accepting that I felt low for my own hidden thoughts. If he only knew my purpose for being in his quaint little town, how friendly would he have been then?

Among other things, I'll bet suicides weren't good for business.

"How much is a room?" I asked.

For the first time, the young man's eyes wandered up then down. There was no contempt in his voice or expression when he spoke, "First night's free, and so is Christmas. After that we can talk."

"But—"

"Let me show you to your room. You probably want to clean up before dinner."

"I—" I never got to finish the statement because the blond man was already walking toward the stairs. Lamely, I followed.

"I've got some clothes here from a man who forgot his luggage a few months back," the innkeeper offered. "I'll bet you could find something in them that would fit."

"Thank you," I said as I followed him down a wide hallway on the second floor. At the very end of the corridor I could see a bathroom, brightly decorated with pink towels and a peach shower curtain. He led me to the last of three oak doors on the right.

"Here you go," he said, swinging the door open. The room was fabulous. A colorful vase sat between two windows and the foot of the bed. A beautiful fern rose majestically from its soil all the way to the ornate metal ceiling high above. The four corners of the double bed were marked with thick mahogany posts, topped with pineapple carvings. The carpeting was a pale blue that matched the pillowcases and the floral comforter. The curtains, also pale blue, were fashioned of a fine lace that allowed the winter sun to shine in. There was a phone on one of the two nightstands, and beside the phone I could see a remote control that I surmised had to do with an electric bed. There was no television in the room.

The innkeeper entered behind me and stepped over to the large armoire. He swung open two doors to reveal a very modern Sony TV hidden within.

"We don't have cable here in Gray, but we're high enough to get eight stations pretty well. As you saw, the bathroom's just outside the door. In a minute, I'll bring in the clothes I mentioned."

"Thank you."

The man winked. "You're very welcome. Isn't this what Christmas is all about?"

He left and returned a few moments later with an armload of dress shirts and casual slacks that looked suspiciously similar to those he was wearing.

I wanted desperately to fill the tub and soak in warm water for hours, but I knew it would have been rude not to accept the dinner that had been so kindly offered. I settled for a sponge bath that left the inn's facecloth embarrassingly dirty. I tried hand washing the rose-colored square of material, but it was no use. I laid the cloth back on the sink and hoped the filth would come out in a machine.

I had shaven one time or another over the past couple of weeks but I really wanted to take off the scruffy beard that had already re-grown. Unfortunately, there were no shaving utensils to be found.

The shirt was my size, or would have been one year before. These days, my undernourished body left much of the material hanging loosely. I didn't fare so well with the pants either. I was forced to roll up the cuffs twice to keep material from dragging on the floor. I was glad, however, that they were longer instead of shorter because I had no other stockings and my white socks had long-since turned a frightful gray-black.

Back in my room, I pulled my worn sneakers back on and went downstairs. It was no problem finding the dining room. I simply followed the sound of a boisterous voice.

There were eight people sitting around a formally set table. The innkeeper sat at the far end, next to a soft-spoken, pretty brunette woman that I judged to be his wife. To the right of the couple was a hefty elderly gent. His bright red nose and cheeks were likely a testament to a tipping hobby. Beside the elderly man sat two pre-teen boys, who appeared content but strangely subdued. They had the same long hawk nose as the older man, though of course lacked the bright veins. Across from them was a middle-aged couple who apparently had been the cause of the commotion I had been hearing. From the way the salt-and-pepper man kept using the terms "in this part of the country" and "what beautiful views" I assumed he and his wife were tourists of one fashion or another. Sitting at the other end of the table, exactly opposite the innkeeper was a strange little girl. She was young, maybe eight or nine. Her neck hung at an awkward angle and her left arm was twisted in such a way that her palm faced outward even when hanging in a relaxed position.

There was an empty chair and a place setting between the girl and the tourists. Feeling awkward, I moved across the room and settled down.

"It's nice to have you with us," the innkeeper said. "I'm Pat Olsen and this is Carolyn, my wife."

"I'm Skip Ralstat."

The others also introduced themselves. The little girl had an especially difficult time saying her own name, "Juuu...dii...tth Aaa...nnne."

"Judith Ann is our guest of honor tonight," the innkeeper said. "She's from the St. John's Children's Center here in town. We have one of the children over for dinner every night. It just happens that her turn fell on this beautiful Christmas Eve."

I looked to the girl. She was beaming, so obviously ecstatic at being here. These people, the innkeeper and his wife, had to have been cut from a very special cloth. I felt a deep respect for them.

The roast beef dinner and its accompaniments were wonderful. Not only were they delicious but they were also were served on beautiful blue chintz china. The drinks came in elegant rose and cobalt colored glasses. I did find it of interest that only juice, milk and water were offered with our meal. I wondered if maybe the innkeeper or his wife was a recovering alcoholic, but I somehow doubted it.

It may have been that they didn't drink on this occasion so as not to tempt the old man with the red face. He looked as though the last thing he needed was more alcohol to drink. As it was, the veins on his nose looked red and swollen to the bursting point.

I didn't speak more than a few sentences

during the meal. The tourist and his wife did most of the talking, though the innkeeper seemed to have a way of inserting himself just enough to keep the man from becoming boorish.

Sitting across from the somewhat somber boys, it was now obvious to me that the girl made them uncomfortable. As is often the way, the healthy fear those who are less healthy. It's almost as if we fear what we may become. In the boys' cases, maybe they really did believe that somehow the girl's condition was contagious.

Though he'd didn't utter as much as one word to them, or to anyone else for that matter, the old man kept looking toward the boys and grunting. For their part, other than furtive glances toward the girl, the boys didn't look at anyone at all.

Though the food was delicious, I was unable to finish my second plate. Apparently, my stomach had shrunk considerably over the last year. As much as I wanted to, I couldn't have eaten another bite.

I excused myself and pushed away from the table. "Could you wake me around nine?" I asked as I crossed the room.

"Sure," the innkeeper said.

With only a few hours of life left to me, I was afraid that my mind wouldn't let my body sleep but it turned out to be no problem at all. In a very short time, the soft pillow and the equally soft bed dragged me into a deep, coma-like sleep.

Chapter Nine

The End of Everything

When the innkeeper knocked at nine, I woke easily. I felt rested even though I had only slept for a few hours. He knocked a second time. "Thank you," I said loudly enough that he could hear me through the closed door.

"An envelope came for you," he said. "I'll just slide it under the door."

An envelope for me? I imagined that the waitress had returned the tip. How she'd known I was here I didn't know, but it was a small town. Probably every resident of Gray knew about me by now.

I sat up and swung my legs over the bed, smiling because the ripped sneakers were still on my feet. I hadn't bothered to get undressed at all. Months of living in the streets had certainly changed my living habits. There had been a time that I wouldn't have gone to bed with anything on but pajamas, and not even then until I had brushed my teeth and rinsed my mouth with mouthwash. Even though I did carry a toothbrush in the breast pocket of my worn jacket, I had recently been known to go for a week without brushing, and my body had not seen the inside of a set of pajamas in almost a year.

Things certainly had changed.

I looked down at myself and knew I would have to give back the clothes that had been loaned to me. It wouldn't have been right to ruin them at the bottom of the ravine. I started to unbutton the shirt, then thought better of it.

What would the innkeeper think if I went strolling out into the night in my dirty cloths? He would surely wonder why I was leaving so soon. He might even be suspicious enough to call the police. Then what would I do? No, the best way would be to change into my old clothes at the bridge, just before I took my final plunge. At least that way the innkeeper could reclaim his clothes.

I buttoned the shirt again, then wrapped my old pants around me waist, stuffing just enough of them into my belt to hold them in place. Then I pulled on my trench coat and pushed my dirty shirt inside one sleeve of my jacket. I buttoned up and modeled for myself in the dresser mirror. Yes, I did look a little thicker, but considering how my body had dwindled over the last year, I doubted anyone would find my appearance strange. I started to leave, but then thought of one more task.

I took the last of my money out and laid it on the dressing stand beside the bed. A little under ten dollars was the best I could do to return the favor, but at least it was something.

As I turned to leave I saw the envelope that had been thrust under the door. I'd nearly forgotten about the returned money. I stooped to pick it up. Written on the face was, 'To Skip', and in the upper left corner was printed, 'THE SANTA SHOP'.

Had I mentioned my name to the

shopkeeper? I must have. But what could he possibly have sent to me? The flap wasn't sealed and I easily was able to pull out the single sheet of folded paper inside. The letterhead across the top read, *The Santa Shop, Gray, Vermont.*

The next line was, *Application for Employment.* The third and last line was a single question followed by a blank line to fill in. It simply read, *Applicant's name?* That was it. That was all there was to the Employment Application for The Santa Shop. No history of employment or addresses were requested. No references of any kind were asked for. Not even the applicant's age. It simply asked for a name? What kind of lunacy was this? *Must have been just a first page*, I thought. I looked at the sheet again. Almost as if in answer to my question I saw, *page 1 of 1* printed in the upper hand corner.

I laid the sheet along with the empty envelope then I left the room. Time was short and the hiring practices of the little Vermont toyshop weren't issues I had time to dwell upon.

"Thank you again for the meal," I said as I passed by the dining room. The others were still gathered and I could hear the tourist again reciting how beautiful the views were.

"You're leaving?" came the innkeeper's voice.

"Thought I'd go for a walk."

"Better button up. It gets cold around here."

"I will."

It was dark, and the air had a biting edge even more harsh than the air in Albany. I took a deep breath and thought it might have been the freshness of it that made it seem colder. There was no smog, no acid rain, not even noise pollution. I pulled my collar tight and felt glad to have the padding of my old clothes as insulation against the night.

The walk to the river was quicker than I remembered it. Was my mind speeding my perceptions along? I thought my life was supposed to flash slowly before me just before death, but possibly that was only when the final act became irreversible. Maybe my subconscious wanted to change my mind, to make me think I needed more time to get it all straight.

"It won't work," I whispered as I approached the ravine and the bridge just beyond. "What I want isn't important. This is for Tabitha and for Derek."

I almost expected a supernatural response, but none came. The night was silent, save for the whisper of wind through bare trees and the barely audible splashing sounds that came from the sluggish black water far below.

Dreading every minute of it, I pulled my coat off and quickly traded the innkeeper's clothes for my own. The skin of my arms and legs was numb before the job was complete and I was able to pull my trench coat back on.

For the longest time, with my hands stuffed deeply into my pockets and my chin buried in the collar of my jacket, I stood there at the edge of the bridge and waited for the tremors to subside. After a while, I realized that it wasn't the cold that raced in arcs just below my flesh. It was the pulse of my own fear.

Intellectually, I had not found it hard to come to this decision. My body, however, seemed in these last few moments to take offense at the idea. I could feel self-preservation ringing like an incessant fire alarm in my chest. On one level, I wanted nothing so much as to scream out for help, to find a way out of this inevitable fate my thoughts had pinned onto my body. My cruel thoughts, however, had other things in mind. I had been responsible for the death of two wonderful people. Some-one had to pay for that.

I left the borrowed clothing in a pile at the edge of the bridge where it met the paved road, and I forced myself to move forward. My muscles felt weak, barely controllable. I took two then three steps. My heart pounded and my limbs vibrated. It was hard to explain but I felt as though I was placing my head in the mouth of a cannon. It became obvious that the human body was not made for self-sacrifice. The body wants to live. It will fight you to live.

The cold wind tore at me but it was nothing compared to the winds of terror that racked my insides. Internal alarms and whistles were ringing, driving gales of terror across every nerve in my body. My flesh desperately wanted to live.

I forced myself to move forward another ten feet. It appeared phase two of our body's self-defense mechanism was a lying mind. Suddenly, hundreds, even thousands of reasons for continuing to live exploded inside my head. I could hear an entire debating team presenting one argument after the other, all in favor of staying alive, all in favor of getting away from this bridge. Some of the arguments seemed reasonable, but others like, *You've got to finish your* Pop-Tarts™, weren't nearly so convincing.

By the time I had gone a full twenty feet more, my mind had become a raging battle-field of dialog and my body the recipient of horrific fear-chemical attacks. I struggled to keep the internal vision of the two caskets that held the lifeless bodies of Tabitha and Derek in my mind. I knew I was doing this for them, to pay for my grievous crime. As long as I kept their dead images in front of me I knew I could do this.

Suddenly, as I stood there maybe thirty feet onto the bridge now, the whistles the bells and all the shivers stopped. It was as if the self-preservation switch had been suddenly toggled back off, rendered useless by the sheer hopelessness of it all. And it was then, while my mind was silent, that I became the most tempted to turn and run. It would have been so easy to back away from my commitment, so easy to leave my dead family in the past. In this same silence, I learned that even my mind wanted to live. Life was a precious thing, not to be given up at the whim of a dream or in the heat of emotion.

"Which is why I have to do it," I told myself as I grabbed hold of the steel rail. The frosty cold steel burned like fire.

"I need to endure the same loss that they did," I said aloud.

A vision of them again in their last moments during the fire came to my mind. I saw her desperate struggle to reach his crib, and I watched as both of them succumbed to the thick smoke that surrounded them. I wanted to scream out for her, to scream, *I'll save you, I'll save you both.* But, I couldn't. No one could. No one could bring those two people who I had loved so much back to life. I had killed them as surely as if I had started that fire myself.

The scene was so clear, so horrifying, that I knew I could and would go through with this. I owed them that much. I owed them retribution for my failure to be there. I owed them my life.

I leaned out heavily and looked down into the ravine. Though a partial moon was out, its light was unable to penetrate all the way to the ice and water that I could hear swirling angrily below.

I stepped onto the lowest rung of the railing and grabbed hold of a large, vertical, steel support. The ice-cold rivets burned like hot buttons in my palm. There was a second horizontal bar above the first. And above that was the railing itself. Perfect, really, for this sort of activity, like a small ladder of death.

I took two deep breaths and lifted my other foot onto the bottom rung. I could feel the fear leaching out of me like an excised demon. In moments, my thoughts fell silent. I was an empty husk. Maybe the life, the very soul of me had already fled. Maybe all that was left was this useless, guilty body that had only one last job to do.

I held tight to the cold support and lifted my right foot to the second rung. Wind whipped across the bridge, threatening to hurl me forward into the lecherous maw of the ravine. For a fraction of a second, terror reared up inside me again. I threw my weight back against the gale and held on with a clamp-like grip, one hand on the rail and the other on the higher support.

Then, as suddenly as it had come, the wind died down again. My fear subsided but it took a while longer for my hands to relax their strangleholds on the steel. Feeling ridiculous, I hung there, half on, half off the bridge. Suddenly, the debating team returned to its task. Arguments in defense of my life swelled and roared in a chaotic swirl. I knew I was ready for this, ready to pay my penance, but still I clung to life.

I forced a vision of Tabitha and Derek upon myself again. I saw their deaths in the smoke and their dual caskets. I imagined Tabby, impatient and accusatory in her death. The debating team fled again, unable to function with the obvious gilt of the blood I had caused right before them. Finally, once again, my mind fell silent.

Now was the time to jump.

Now!

Taking one last gulp of brutally cold air, I took another step up the rail. I faced the ravine and flexed my legs for the final two steps that would carry me into oblivion.

"Wait!" The man's voice was powerful and commanding.

My body and mind were tempered for the leap. Knowing there was little that he or anyone could do to stop me, I turned my head and looked for curiosity's final sake.

Though the moon was far from full, I could see the figure approaching slowly along the bridge. His gait was slow and methodical, almost somber. He was dressed entirely in black, and the folds of a black hood hid his face. As he drew closer, the breath caught in my throat.

It wasn't a dark pantsuit he wore. The man was garbed in a robe, monk style. His hood, too, seemed to be part of the same medieval outfit. Though I wasn't an especially superstitious person, my heart pounded at the thought that this might be death himself. The Grim Reaper had come for me.

"It would be wise to step down from there," he said softly, stopping a comfortable twenty feet from me.

I could see small puffs of vapor emerge from the hood with each of his words, which relieved me to some extent. At least he was human. Possibly demented, I thought, but human nonetheless.

"Who are you?" I asked, still gripping the steel support and rail like a monkey.

"I'm you," the man said. "Or a man very like you."

"What are you doing here?"

"I came for you. I was perched in that same spot two years ago. I knew you would be here."

"How?"

"One of us always comes. It's almost a law of nature."

"You can't stop me from jumping."

"No. You're right about that. I can't. Fortunately, I don't have to."

"You mean you don't care if I jump?"

"No, what I mean is you won't jump."

I jerked my head to look out over the ravine. My body was tensed. I knew I could have done it then. Something held me back, though. I tried to recall that same vision of my wife and child, but it wouldn't come. The mystery of this man was clouding my thoughts.

I decided to continue talking. What difference would a few minutes make? I stepped down and returned my feet to the concrete and my hand from the rail, but when I tried to pull my hand away from the vertical support, the skin of my palm ripped painfully. The cold had welded it to the steel.

"You ought to warm those in your pockets before you get frostbite," the man said.

I laughed half-heartedly. "The last thing I need to worry about is frostbite."

The man pulled his hood down to reveal a clean-shaven face and worry lines that placed him five or ten years ahead of me. His hair was dark and full. There was a gentle smile on his face that reminded me of the toy shopkeeper and Barwood and even of Father Johnston....

I knew I had the keys to a mystery in my hand, but I couldn't quite fit all the pieces together just yet. The priest, Barwood, the toy shopkeeper, and now the Grim Reaper were somehow all connected, but I couldn't say how or why.

My hand darted to my breast pocket. Yes, my truck was still there. Like a little boy, I squeezed it and felt a sense of relief.

"I'll be leaving Gray tonight," the man told me. "It's my time to go."

"Yeah, mine too," I said with a chuckle. "In a manner of speaking, anyway."

"You'll like Gray," he said. "The people here are friendly, and they understand us."

"You keep talking as though we're both members of some club."

He smiled and nodded. "I guess you could say we are. You might call us The Suicide Club. Or maybe Christmas Leap Brothers would be a better term."

"You still didn't tell me who you are."

"That remains to be seen. To be honest, I'm

not entirely sure of that. I only know that I'm not the same person who hung from that rail two years ago."

"Why didn't you?" I asked.

He paused and stared at me for the longest time.

"Jump, you mean."

"Yeah."

"I'm not sure I could answer that in any way that you'd understand right now, but someone just like me showed up."

"Did he talk you out of it?"

He grinned again. "No one could have talked me out of it. But he did make me think."

"Was he another one of *us*?" I asked sarcastically.

"Yes, he was a Santa."

"A Santa?"

"You'll know in a day or two what all this means. Jarod will explain everything."

"Jarod?"

"Yes, Jarod from The Santa Shop."

"I think I should get on with it," I said, nodding toward the railing.

"I suppose you should. We both should." He

pulled his black hood back up over his head.

I reached over to grab the rail and winced as my tender hand came in contact with the steel. I tried to take my eyes from the unusual stranger, but the black outfit gave him a disconcerting aura. With the hood up, I couldn't seem to shake the feeling that he really was the deliverer of death. Maybe he had come to make sure that I did jump. Then he could steal my soul as it fled my drowned body.

As I stared at him, I realized he wore the perfect outfit for communicating with a pre-suicide victim. Who better to keep one on the edge and maybe a little too scared to die?

"I left a bag for you," the reaper said in a commanding voice, quite unlike the one he used when his hood was down. He raised an arm to point, and the material of his loose sleeves created the illusion of a bat's wing. "There."

I looked to where he pointed and I could see the silhouette of something sitting at the edge of the road. *Another trick*, I thought. He could be trying to pique my curiosity, anything to keep me from jumping. Well it wasn't going to work. I didn't need to know what was in that bag. I didn't.

As he began walking toward me, his long robe dragged on the snow and gave me the impression that he was actually floating. I hurriedly stepped to the first rung of the rail, but I need not have bothered. The stranger crossed over toward the opposite railing, and gave me a wide berth. He continued on past.

Spellbound, I watched him drift to the other end of the bridge, furthest from town. He stopped and looked toward me.

"Hurry," he said. "Open the case. The children are waiting, Santa. They're waiting for you."

And suddenly the reaper was gone.

Stupidly, I stepped back down but continued to cling to the railing. I tried to piece together some reality from all this. Had he been real or simply imagined? I thought I knew for a while there, but it all felt so damned impossible.

My body shuddered involuntarily. How close had I come to an evil death? How near had I been to losing the only thing I still possessed—my soul?

I didn't know who he was. And I didn't expect that I ever would. Maybe he was just a man, but then again maybe he wasn't. My body suddenly began trembling with uncontrollable fear. My knees weakened and I fell to the concrete.

What was I supposed to do then? They were dead, and I wasn't. I didn't want to be alone, and I didn't want them to be dead.

I did the only thing I could then, I sobbed. I sobbed from the deepest most pure place in my soul. I sobbed for my family and I sobbed for myself. I sobbed for all the Christmas Eves that my family would never see, and I sobbed for all the life I had lost this past year.

I'd always known that I had to go on, but I didn't want to. I didn't want to leave them in the ground alone. And I didn't dare to go on in life without them. This suicide mission of mine had just been a way to escape the hard journey that life had taken me through. I had to get up now, I had to move on, and I had to find some justification for staying alive.

When the worst of my fear subsided, I knew

that jumping was out of the question. Not only was it wrong, but I just couldn't shake the feeling that he was waiting for me down there, waiting to whisk my soul into the brutal underworld.

I got unsteadily to my feet.

What now? I thought. Where would I go? What would I do? Suddenly, I remembered the case he had left for me. I almost expected to find spiders, snakes or scorpions in there. Maybe it would be eye of newt and wing of bat.

I stumbled back to solid land, toward whatever he had left. It was a simple black suitcase, about the size of a carry-on flight bag. It stood beside the clothes that I had piled in the snow. Fearful but curious, I dropped to my knees and tipped the case on its side. There was a single zipper, which I gently pulled. When the bag didn't blow up, I unzipped it the rest of the way and lifted the flap.

The material was shockingly bright and cheerful, especially considering the gloom that I'd been experiencing over the last hour, not exactly the Christmas Eve I had originally planned. I smiled and put the red hat with white trimming on my head.

Feeling foolish, I donned the rest of Kris Kringle's outfit. There was even a pair of black boots and warm black mittens. Near the bottom of the case, I found a stick-on cotton beard and a single sheet of white paper. The black letters of the invitation were bold and clear:

DEAR SANTA:

You are welcome to visit us at Saint John's Children's Center. We look forward to seeing you again this year.

Sincerely,

The letter was signed by a dozen young hands, and at the very bottom of the page was a sentence written by an adult hand, "The presents you delivered earlier are waiting in the foyer."

I read the invitation several times and thought about Judith Ann, whom I had met at the bed and breakfast. How many needy children just like her were depending on Santa Claus to show up tonight?

I glanced back at the bridge but could see

no sign of the Reaper. He hadn't even waited to see whether or not I had jumped. Instead, he had just left his case and walked away. There was nobody else to fill the suit. I had effectively been trapped into playing this part. It was either that or disappoint a group of children who I knew had already lived through more than enough disappointment.

I had to do it.

The lack of choice made me angry. No longer in control of my own fate, I felt as though a great hand had scooped me up and thrown me against the winds of my life. I stuffed the innkeeper's clothes into the empty bag and made my way back towards town. By the time I came into a view of the Main Street, my hands had thawed just enough to ache severely. In a way, it was good that the Santa suit came with gloves, otherwise, I would have been handing out children's presents spotted with blood.

I knew I could have gone back to the bed and breakfast for directions, but Gray was such a small town that I figured the children's center wouldn't take long to find. It turned out that I was right.

There were a total of five streets that intersected and ran roughly perpendicular to the Main Street. River Road was one. I had only to walk a short way down two more before I found the center. It was a two-story brick affair with a short steeple on the front. Someone had obviously been watching out for me because the front door opened as I approached.

A young brunette woman opened the door. She had the most beautiful smile. Welcome to Saint John's Children Center, Santa," she said to me. "My name is Karen. Would you come this way?"

She ushered me into a wide dim corridor with a high ceiling. A series of three incandescent bulbs barely lit our way as she led me toward the double doors at the far end of the hall. A could hear quite a bit of commotion coming from the other side of the doors.

"Good luck, Santa," Karen mouthed as she

opened both doors and stepped back to make way for me. The sounds I had heard only moments before were gone. The space beyond the door was black.

I looked to my guide. She nodded and gave me that beautiful smile again, then gestured toward the blackness of the room before me.

Cautiously, I walked forward.

"Surprise, Santa!" a chorus of voices rang out.

Suddenly, bright-colored lights sprang on, illuminating one of the most gorgeous Christmas trees I had ever seen. At least twenty feet from base to peak, the tree rose up in a full and perfect cone. The lights must have been painstakingly strung around the tree's limbs because I couldn't see even one place where two lights of the same color twinkled side-by-side. Hanging from the tips of the branches were all manner of ornaments. There was everything from glittering balls of glass to paper drawings of Santa and his elves. A beautiful life-like angel doll with gauze wings stared down at me from the very tip of the twinkling evergreen.

"Do you like it?" a young voice asked from

somewhere to the side of me. I had been so overcome by the sight of the tree that until now I hadn't noticed the gaggle of children that were crowed in a semi-circle around it.

"It's wonderful," I said, feeling a familiar rush of appreciation for the spirit of the season. I turned to the children and examined their ranks; they were an unusual bunch, many deformed in body. A twisted and limp arm here, a braced leg there, wheelchairs and crutches were only some of the medical accessories I saw in use. One unfortunate boy was secured tightly to a stainless steel frame that resembled nothing so much as a medieval stretching machine. His arms and legs were fully outstretched and strapped with wide black straps to the glorified bed apparatus. A male nurse was tilting the bed as upright as it would go. I watched as he locked it in place at something more than a forty-five degree angle, but quite a bit less than fully upright. The boy's dark eyes squinted, possibly with the pain of the movement, but the happy smile never left his lips.

The same amazing life-filled grins were

spread across the rest of the youthful faces as well. Even though these children had been given some of the hardest lots in life, there wasn't a Christmas sourpuss in the bunch.

"Ho, ho, ho," I said in my deepest voice, sorry only that I had been too stubborn to practice on my way here. "Meeerry Christmas!"

"Can we do presents now?" the boy from the tilted bed asked. His voice was tight, almost shrill. I looked at the wide straps that held his chest and stomach to the bed and thought it wondrous that he could speak at all.

"Of course we can open presents," I said to him, "and I bet I've got a good one for you."

"And me, Santa?" an older girl said. Her head seemed strangely out of shape, as though one side was swollen. Her left eye was puffy, as well.

"And me?"

"And me?"

"And me—"

"Ho, ho, yes," I said, hoping the man from the bridge had been truthful with me when he said the children's gifts were waiting for me. It would never ever have wanted to disappoint a single one of these children.

"I have presents for everyone."

"Are you going to open the ones we gave to you?"

"You bet I am," I said. "Opening presents is my second favorite thing to do."

"What's your first?" one of the children asked.

"Ho, ho, ho. Giving them, of course."

The children broke into a raucous fit of giggles and conversation.

Chapter Ten

Moving On

Two years later, I crouched in the bushes off to the side of the bridge. I wanted to make sure that the newest Santa didn't try to jump again. He was a good man, a forest ranger from northern Maine. His trek to the bridge had been particularly grueling. I'm told he walked more than half the way, several hundred miles in all. My predecessor had chosen him well.

It was hard to explain all the emotions that had whirled back and forth across Christmas Leap that night. But it hadn't been easy on either of us. I knew what a difficult master guilt could become, and I desperately wanted to help ease this man's pain. But I also knew that healing had to come ultimately from inside his own heart. I could only give him the direction, but it was he who had to make the journey. I felt confident that he would, and tonight the first steps had been taken.

I hadn't so much talked him down as hinted at my own story and told him how I had come to survive my own aborted Christmas Leap. When all the words had been said, I left him there on the bridge, just as I had been left those two years before.

Of course, as I'd known, he stopped sobbing after a time and went to retrieve the case I'd left. Saint John's Children's Center would soon have a visit from the newest Santa.

As we had discussed, Karen waited until she saw him walk up the drive to the children's hospital, then she drove across the bridge to meet me. I had already removed the black robe and hood and had left them in a cloth bag beside the bridge for David to pick up in a few hours.

"All packed?" I asked as I slid into the passenger's seat and closed the door.

"You bet? It's all in the back."

I pushed over right beside her and kissed

her solidly on the lips. Fortunately, she hadn't started the car moving yet.

"Do we neck or do we drive?" she managed to say amid my affectionate mauling.

"All right," I said in mock sadness and pushed over just barely enough for her to turn the steering wheel freely. "I guess we drive."

"Where to, Santa?"

I took my little truck from my pocket and rolled it gently back and forth across my knee. "Albany," I said. "I think we'll pay my friend Jenny a visit."

"She sounds nice."

"She is. I'm hoping she needs a couple of partners in her corner store."

"Fine by me," Karen giggled. "But I run the cash."

...and she did for many years to come.

WITH ALL GOD'S BLESSINGS, A VERY MERRY CHRISTMAS TO YOU!

About the Author

Tim Greaton has been writing since age seven. It is hoped that some thirty-one years later, his work has improved somewhat. His fiction and non-fiction works have previously appeared in both national and regional magazines and in newspapers across the northeast. Hundreds of pages of his advertising work are still in use on the Internet today. Tim now resides in southern Maine with his wife, three children, a few cats and hundreds of ducks who stubbornly refuse to migrate. Even as you read these words, Tim is hard at work on his next novel, as yet to be titled, due out this coming year.